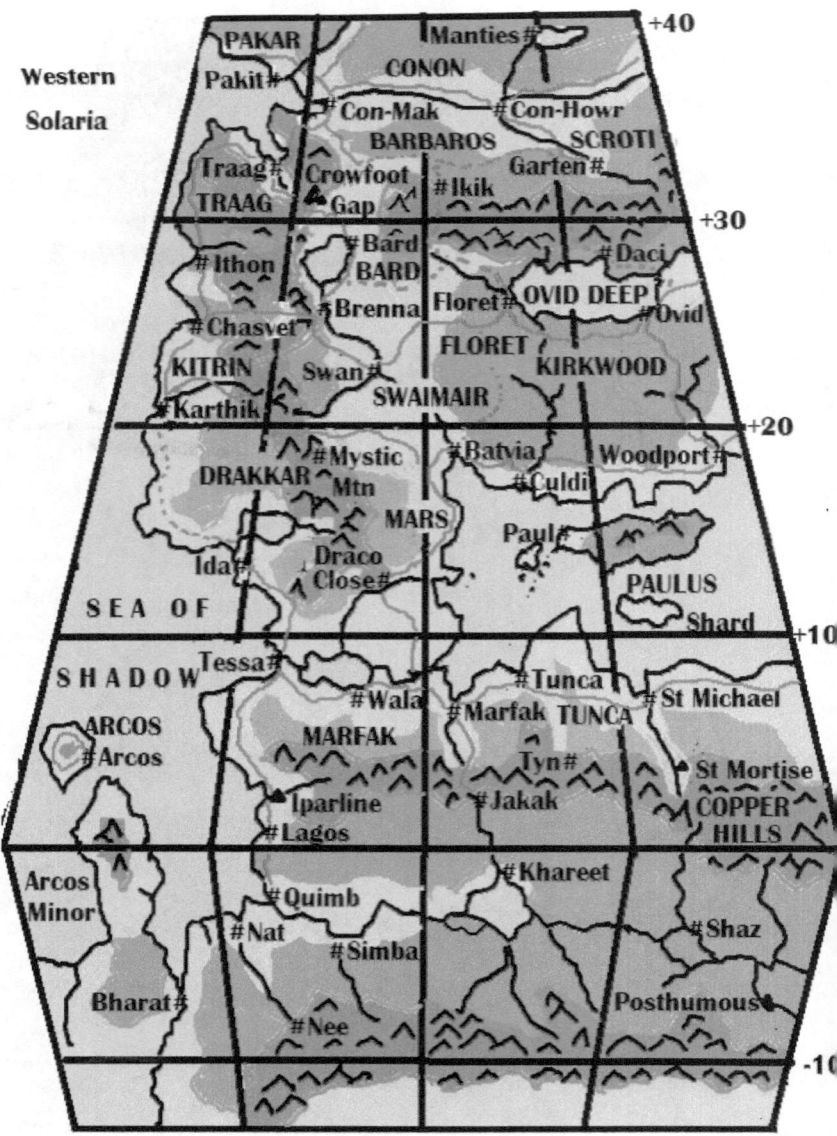

Western Solaria

+40

PAKAR
Pakit#

Manties#

CONON

#Con-Mak   #Con-Howr

BARBAROS   SCROTI

Traag#   Crowfoot   Garten#
TRAAG   Gap   #Ikik

+30

#Ithon   #Bard   #Daci
              BARD
#Chasvet   #Brenna   Floret# OVID DEEP
                                          #Ovid
KITRIN   Swan#   FLORET
#Karthik   SWAIMAIR   KIRKWOOD

+20

              #Mystic   #Batvia   Woodport#
DRAKKAR   Mtn   #Culdi
              MARS
              Draco   Paul#
Ida#   Close#
                                      PAULUS
SEA OF   Shard

+10

SHADOW   Tessa#
                        #Tunca
ARCOS   #Wala   #Marfak   #St Michael
#Arcos   MARFAK   TUNCA
                        Tyn#   St Mortise
            Iparline   #Jakak   COPPER
            #Lagos   HILLS

Arcos   #Khareet
Minor
            #Quimb   #Shaz
            #Nat   #Simba
Bharat#   Posthumous#
            #Nee

-10

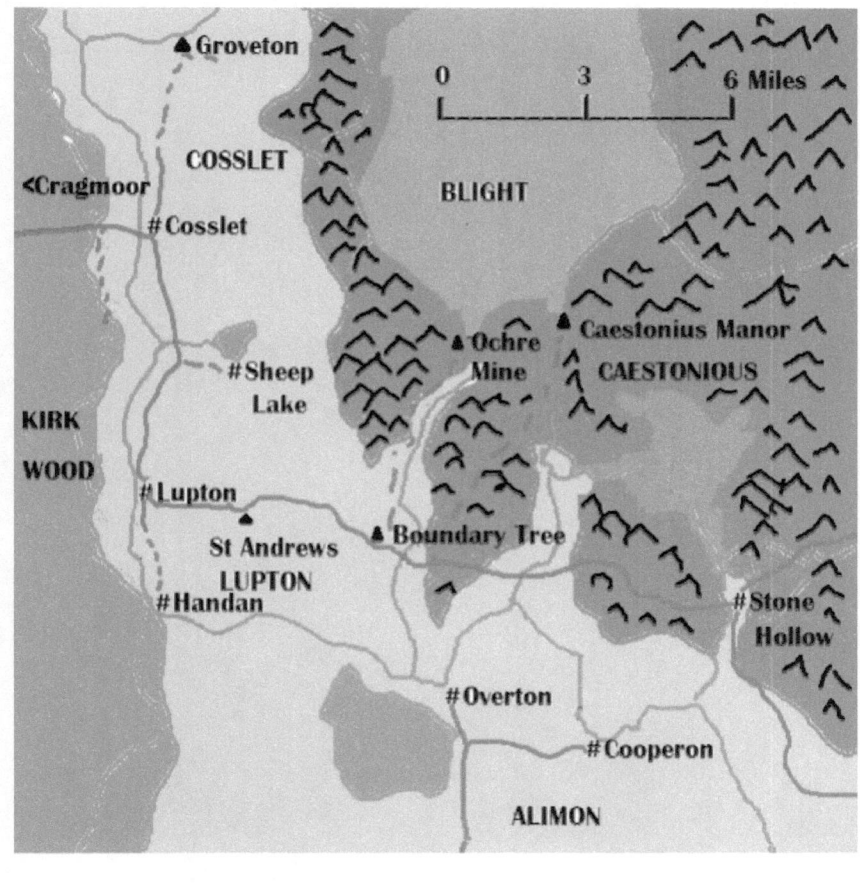

Empire: Country

Empire, Volume 1

Tim Goff

Published by Tim Goff, 2022.

EMPIRE: COUNTRY

First edition. October 12, 2022.

Copyright © 2022 Tim Goff.

ISBN: 979-8985988987

Written by Tim Goff.

Also by Tim Goff

Table of Contents

EMPIRE: COUNTRY I - Tia

"Sir, please grant us shelter." A sneeze threatened to erupt through Tia's nose as she spoke the words.

"No." Beady eyes lost in a tangle of facial hair glared at Tia.

"Ah-choo!" The sneezes violence made Tia's slight body curl despite the sodden mass of her dress. "I shall inform Master Brutus of your inhospitality."

"The orders come from him." The window banged shut.

"Wretched peasants." Sir Peter Cortez reached for his sword hilt. "Who are they, to refuse shelter to their betters?"

Tia placed a restraining hand on the knight's arm. "Don't bother, Sir Cortez. We depart this place at once. Kyle!" The last word was directed at a huge man whose cask-like body strained at a long blue jacket

"Yes, my lady." Kyle lifted her without apparent effort and trudged across the yard, boots making sucking sounds with each step.

Once in the cart, Tia huddled against her maid Rebecca while Kyle heaved himself onto the driver's bench.

The wain lurched into motion and almost collided with a pair of figures in clerical cassocks. Tia glimpsed a wrinkled female face fringed by gray hair. "Beware," said the priestess as the wagon rolled past, along with other words lost in the cacophony of pounding rain and rumbling wheels.

Wonderful. The priestess was probably warning them of bandits. The roads swarmed with the vermin these days.

The knight rode alongside the wagon. "Sir Peter, how far to the next shelter?"

"The old monastery is two miles from here."

"Will the monks permit us shelter?" Tia reached the wagon. Another sneeze threatened to escape. *Two miles. Half an hour on this miserable road.*

"It's abandoned."

'Abandoned' didn't sound hopeful. But at this point, Tia was ready to commandeer the next barn, shack, or wild animal den they came across, so long as it was dry.

The wagon lurched sideways. Tia slammed into Rebecca. "Kyle, must you strike every chuckhole?"

Auburn hair peeped from beneath Rebecca's hood as she straightened herself. "It's alright, my lady."

"No, it's not alright," said Tia. "Thanks to his piss poor driving," she jabbed her index finger into the oafs back, "my nice dry carriage is back at Stone Hollow with a broken axle."

The wagon rumbled through a corner. Bramble and weeds stretched into the distance on either side of the road. Ahead, the road dipped into a gully with a plank bridge at the low point.

God above, what a depressing place. I need a hit of Dust. Tia's hand crept towards her hidden jacket pocket. *Just one little hit to tide me over until I'm someplace warm and dry with a decent bottle of wine at hand.*

Sir Peter's steed appeared alongside the wagon. His gauntleted hand motioned at a spiky shape that leaned over the highway on the gorges opposite side. "That's the Boundary Tree, my lady – the border between Cosslet, Lupton, and Caestoninus baronies."

Tia squinted at the tree. Brown-robed figures and half a dozen head of cattle huddled beneath its branches. Peasants, not bandits.

The tree vanished from view as the road dropped towards a bridge almost submerged beneath the orange-tinted water. "Ochre Creek," said Sir Peter. "It's tainted by the old mines north of here."

Tia didn't care about worthless pits in the ground. She just hoped the wretched bridge didn't collapse.

The cart's wheels struck the bridge with a jolt and took on a hollow sound. Then they were across, and Ginger began towing the conveyance up the far slope.

"My lady, we should reach Cosslet Castle before nightfall," said Peter.

Tia suppressed a groan. Peter's half-brother Ian was suitor number four on 'the list.'

Tia sighed. Marriage was such a bother! But her parents were determined to attain aristocratic rank, which meant their offspring – specifically Tia, as her brother was much too young – had to find nobles willing to marry beneath their station. Alas, most such aristocrats possessed flawed bodies, flawed characters, or both. Plus, they were all in debt to their eyeballs. No doubt Baron Cortez hoped for a handsome dowry to settle his pile of bills.

A gust of wind blew rain into Tia's eyes and turned the world into a watery blur. Worse, the dampness had reached her hair. *My curls will be ruined. How can I make a good first impression on the bumpkin Baron if my hair is a mess?* She plucked at her sodden coat. *Not to mention the rest of me. Perhaps we can stay overnight at an inn.* The thought made her shudder. Previous roadhouses boasted poor food, coarse company, and bedbugs. Such rude accommodations were suitable only for the lower orders.

Another jolt snapped Tia from her reverie. *We've stopped.* Had the empire's worst driver managed to break yet another wheel? Tia opened her mouth for a retort. Sir Peters outthrust hand filled her vision.

"My lady, stay in the cart." The knight's helm rotated as he surveyed the landscape. Naked steel slick with water gleamed in his fist.

Kyle's bulk tensed. His beefy hand reached beneath the bench.

"What happened?" Nerves made Tia's voice shrill. "Bandits?" Tia's gaze swept from side to side, but the liquid veil remained impenetrable. Brush. Rocks. Weeds. Ahead, the giant oak branches drooped over the road. She blinked. The branches hung at the wrong angle. Queer mounds blocked the highway.

Sir Peter edged his steed closer to the tree.

The Oaf rose to his feet, short sword in hand. "My lady, you might have to run."

"Kyle, what are you talking about?" Tia's heart sounded louder than the rain. A horrid realization penetrated her awareness. A scream fought its way from her throat.

EMPIRE: COUNTRY II - Peter

Peters' stomach clenched as he surveyed the carnage. He'd seen worse, during the war. Hell, he'd done worse, more than once, without a twinge of regret. He'd even jested about it afterward with his fellow knights. This was different. The agency behind this slaughter was inhuman, bestial.

This sort of thing wasn't supposed to happen in the Empire. Not anymore.

Two dead cows and woman lay dead in the road. More bodies hung from the overhead branches like overripe fruit. The pale head and torso of a smooth-faced youngster hung towards the ground from one fork. A pair of legs in black breeches dangled from another. Dark blotches marred the victim's visible skin. All slain in the few score heartbeats he'd been in the gorge.

Peter rotated his head, searching for the perpetrator. Whoever-whatever had killed the peasants must still be close at hand. But where? Apart from the gorge, the terrain was not quite level, covered with knee-high brush. No other trees. Few large boulders. Plenty of hiding spots – for men. But men weren't behind this carnage. Of that, he was certain.

A Demon. The thought struck Peter like a physical blow as images of sorcerous atrocities from the war flashed through his mind – the grisly aftermaths of summoning rituals, and mangled corpses left behind by rampaging demons. This scene mirrored those visions.

It can't be. We killed every sorcerer, every scribe, every priest, and every noble. We burned their books to black ash and scattered the remnants on the wind. We smashed every idol and every altar. They're gone. But this scene said otherwise.

Could the warehouse louts be connected to this massacre? Those wardens possessed brutish natures. But wholesale slaughter? No. But he'd seen fear in the eyes of their spokesman. They knew something. He was sure of it.

Movement caught Peter's attention. Kyle stepped from behind the tree, focused on the muddy ground. Idiot. He should be scanning the area, looking for the assailant. But Kyle was a sorcerer, albeit a pathetic one. Perhaps his magic could provide a clue.

Kyle stepped into the road, still staring at the mud. His head rotated to the side. He straightened.

"Kyle."

Kyle started. His frame shook.

He's spooked. And I can't blame him. But Kyle was a peasant and former legionnaire, born and trained to obedience. "Decurion Kyle, report!"

Kyle turned. "S-Sir."

"Report."

"I-I found tracks." Kyle motioned at a smudged marks on the ground.

Peter leaned in his saddle and peered at a group of smudge marks. They could be tracks. They could also be potholes. *Cousin Charles is the tracker, not me.* "Any idea where it's at?"

Kyle lifted an arm and pointed at an indistinct gap in the shrubbery near the tree. "It took that old road."

The old Ochre Mine Road. Unused for years. "And what might 'it' be?"

"Bearak, I think."

Peter's brow furled beneath his helm. Bearak. Huge savage beasts that occasionally emerged from the nearby Kirkwood to inflict havoc. He remembered Uncle Alexander telling him about a bearak hunt. *'Damn beast tore Trent apart before I could blink. Knocked your daddy right off his feet. Would have gotten him if Sam hadn't put an arrow in its eye.' Uncle Alexander took a swig from his cup. 'We tracked that damn beast for another week. Never did find it again.'*

Peter glanced at the tree, then at the corpses. Bearak's used suckers on tentacles to drain victim's blood. That could account for the marks. The beast's savagery might explain the rest. His tension eased a fraction. Bearak's, despite their fearsomeness, were beasts, not demons. Beasts he could kill. 'Could' being the operative word.

But despite being raised here and fighting an assortment of fearsome creatures in the war, he'd never encountered a bearak.

Peter considered Kyle as he stood stock still in the downpour. How did he know about bearak's? The oaf hailed from civilized Bestia, not the frontier. But he had been posted in the far west, where bearak's were common. "Have you fought a bearak?"

Kyle stared at him. His mouth worked. No words emerged.

"Decurion Kyle, report!"

"I-we fought one, sir." Kyles's face contorted as he spoke. "In Barbaros. It attacked my patrol. It threw Caleb into a tree, tore Jasper apart. We shot arrows at it. It ran."

It threw Caleb into a tree. Peter glanced at the corpses suspended from the branches like monstrous fruit. 'Just like here.' "Move the bodies."

Kyle knelt and grabbed the dead woman's arms. With her hooded black robe and pale scarf, she resembled a cleric.

Peter steered his mount over to the wagon where Tia sat in open-mouthed shock. Her safety mattered more than his. *I failed to save Tessa. I will not fail her sister.*

"Sir Peter." Tia's voice was shrill, bordering on a scream. "Who did this? Are we in danger?"

"Not who, but a what." Peter extended a hand to calm the skittish woman. "A bearak. It's gone now."

Tia grabbed hold of his arm and squeezed tight. "A bearak? Here?"

"From the Kirkwood. It happens on occasion."

"Oh. Let us be gone before it returns." Tia's voice assumed a more authoritative tone. "Lupton must be nearby. We must inform Consul Sigrid of this catastrophe."

"As you wish, my lady." Peter kept the hesitation from his voice. He detested Sigrid. Pompous ass trying to take what wasn't his.

Still, he didn't fool Tia. "Sir Peter, I sense reluctance on your part." *I couldn't fool Tessa, either.*

Rebecca pointed. "My lady, a patrol arrives."

Two rode horses, but the other two moved strangely, they were hunched over, yet their legs made exaggerated up and down motions. Peter blinked. *Bicycles? Here, in the hinterlands?* The two-wheeled contraptions, originally built for military use, were now everywhere. Even here.

"God above, it's a massacre!"

"It's that cursed bearak," said the lead rider. "The wretched beast has fled the Kirkwood.

Peter recognized the gangling figure despite the obscuring rain and hooded cloak. He'd know him anywhere. "Hello, Ian."

The man stared at him. "Peter – is that you?"

"It is me; you stick in the mud." Peter dismounted. "What brings you here?"

Ian motioned at the corpses. "These do. I was visiting Master Vasquez" – he motioned towards a weather-beaten middle-aged man – "when his boy spied ruffians stealing his cattle. He set off in pursuit and I came with him to provide a level head should unpleasantness with Consul Sigrid ensue."

"Pardon my saying, my lord, but this scum got what they deserved." Jason Vasquez's voice was as rough as his visage. "You and I both know they didn't come to my place on their own – Shithead Sigrid or his ass-kisser Kessler sent them, sure as shit. And it ain't the first time; you had Simon Quickhand there"- the farmer pointed at a body draped over a branch – "hauled to you before on charges, and Kessler turned up, smug as dung with his bail." He pointed at the dead woman, now propped against the embankment. "Wanda, another rogue."

Ian winced. "Very true, Jason, but right now I must speak with Peter. Why don't you and your lads beat the bush? I see two dead cows; that leaves nine still out there."

"I will." Vasquez started past Peter, stopped. "You should have stuck that pig-sticker in Sigrid's guts the last time you were here."

Ian's face colored. "Jason, that's enough!"

"Oh, alright." The farmer stumped off, shouting commands to his men.

Ian faced Peter. "You agreed to stay away from here. The last thing I need now is more trouble between myself and Sigrid."

"Don't worry, brother," Peter emphasized the last word, "I shall stay away from Consul Stick-up-his-ass."

"You'd better." Ian's words held no warmth. "Why return here?"

Peter motioned at the wagon. "I am escorting Lady Tia Samos to Cosslet."

Ian glanced at Tia. "She is a looker"-

"She's rich," Peter emphasized the last word.

"I can manage my own affairs."

"And an excellent job you were doing, last time I called. Your creditors claimed all my gains from the war and asked for more. Tell me, have you resorted to selling the family silver yet?"

Ian reeled at Peter's comment. "This isn't the time or the place."

Vasquez stepped from the bushes, a scowl on his face. "Found two more, one dead, the other alive. Got tracks going along the old mine road."

"Cattle or bearak," asked Peter.

"Both."

Ian faced Peter. "Are you up to killing a bearak?"

Peter took a step back. "I am contracted to escort Tia."

"I shall take the young lady to Cosslet." Ian tapped his chest. "I am not entirely unskilled with a blade. And her driver looks like a legion man to me." He motioned at Kyle, who had his nose pressed against the Boundary Tree.

Peter privately judged Ian and Kyle about equal in swordsmanship – competent, but not great. "He is, but"-

"I must call at Castle Lupe and inform Sigrid of this incident."

"Oh." Peter nodded. Ian was right, of course. Ian and Sigrid tolerated one another. "Kyle!"

The big man glanced at him. A dark yet shiny substance clung to his fingers.

"Get in the cart."

Kyle nodded once and plodded across the road.

Ian chattered with Tia at the cart. She, in turn, gave him an appraising eye. Hopefully, that appraisal would be positive.

Tia's voice carried across the rain as she spoke to Ian. "I'd be delighted to accept your offer."

Kyle climbed onto the wagon and flicked the reigns.

Ian paused next to Peter as the cart rumbled past. "Take the bodies to the old monastery. The priests can give the poor bastards last rights."

"I thought that place abandoned."

Ian shook his head. "No, a pair of clerics assumed residence last week. They cleared away the debris and repaired the dormitory." He rode away without waiting for a response.

Peter watched the wagon roll out of sight. Then he turned to Vasquez. "Let's see if we can't find your cows."

EMPIRE: COUNTRY III - Tia

"There, My Lady." The Baron pointed to a fire-blackened ruin surrounded by dead fields dotted with brown and yellow lumps. Just one outbuilding looked even semi-intact. "That's the old Saint Andrews monastery." His lips curled into a frown. "The Scrotti barbarians burned it along with the monks."

It looks awful. And Peter thought to seek shelter there? "How horrid." Butterflies rumbled in Tia's stomach. Most easterners had viewed the Traag War as a distant conflict confined to the half-civilized west. Then thousands of enemy troops erupted from the Kirkwood and carved a bloody swath through Sappho and Cato provinces. It took years to root the vermin from their hidey holes in the Kirkwood. "Surely the Church has plans to rebuild, though?"

The Baron shrugged. "A pair of priests assumed residence." He pointed at a stone building that seemed less damaged than the others. "You can see where they repaired the dormitory."

"I suppose that's a start."

Ian tipped his hat and rode ahead of the cart.

Rebecca leaned close to Tia. "He's the best one yet. Not old, not fat, well mannered, and a cute butt. Grab him."

Tia fought back a giggle and failed. "Well, he doesn't have much hair."

"Buy him a wig."

Tia attempted to picture Ian's narrow face and oversized nose beneath a curled wig. The effort brought on another round of giggles. "He'd look ridiculous." She glanced at the monotonous landscape. "And this place depresses me. It's like the land just died."

"It's autumn." Rebecca's voice turned serious. "There's but one suitor left on the list. If you don't choose one, your parents will. Would you rather marry Lord Lard?"

"Gah, no!" Lord Lard, otherwise known as Sir Osmic, was shorter and wider than Kyle. "He's gross! I'd be crushed should he roll over in his sleep."

"Lord Tombstone?"

"No!" Lord Cassidy resembled an ambulatory corpse, with the disposition to match. He'd expounded on his dead ancestor's accomplishments the entire time she'd been in his gloomy keep that overlooked an even gloomier forest.

"That leaves Lord Pervert."

"Well, Caspar is cute." Tia rubbed her lip. "He dresses well, knows his wines, and he's a rising star in the Navy."

"He also introduced you to his mistress." Rebecca's eyes twinkled. "Remember?"

Tia blushed as she remembered Caspar's graphic proposal. "The Navy will keep him away."

"And in the bed of every harlot around the Mare Imperium," said Rebecca. "I say Baron Cabbage here is a much better prospect than Lord Pervert."

"I could be Baroness Cabbage." The thought held little appeal.

"He's responsible," said Rebecca. "How many other aristocrats would venture into the rain to find missing cattle?"

"Not many." Tia sighed. Rebecca had a point, damn her. Baron Cortez's search for a peasant farmers lost livestock demonstrated an attention to detail lacking in most other aristocrats, but one valued in Equitant. It also showed concern for his subjects – or perhaps their tax revenue. Dead cows meant less income.

Ahead, large mounds resolved themselves into rude huts of twigs and straw. Grubby children and listless adults in brown robes eyed the wagon as they passed.

"Welcome to Lupton," Tia said under her breath.

The wagon clattered across a bridge over a ditch where spikes jutted above brown filth and into a part of town where shops built of dull brick and stone framed a plaza dominated by a fountain with a broken statue in its center.

"Welcome to Lupton's grand market," said Baron Cortez.

Between the cracked stonework and the sagging roofs, the shops resembled sturdier versions of the outlying hovels. The shoddy goods on display and the sullen stares of the proprietors as they passed reinforced this impression. *Not prosperous at all. I'll find few customers here.* Her stated mission was to seek out business opportunities for her family.

Baron Ian guided them past an onion-domed church to a battered gate set in a grim stone edifice with tiny windows near the summit.

A bored teenager in brown leather appeared from a niche. "State yer business." A long spear dangled from his hand.

"Hello Gerald," said the Baron. "Be a good fellow and fetch Consul Sigrid."

The youth appeared uncertain. "I should find Steward Kessler first. His lordships in a terrible snit."

"My words are for Sigrid, not Kessler," said Ian.

The boy winced and vanished inside.

Ian still mounted, leaned over towards Tia. "My pompous fellow aristocrat knows I'm here. But Sigrid enjoys making people wait."

Tia refrained from a sigh. She knew arrogant aristocrats only too well.

Time passed. Tia's fingers caressed the packet of Blue Dust. *I need a hit.*

The gate opened. Gerald reappeared, trailed by a stout, balding man in his early fifties in a cream-colored toga of an eastern traditionalist. "Baron Cortez. What trivial errand brought you to my manor?"

Ian shook his head. "Not so trivial. I just returned from the boundary tree where I found Wanda Schiff, Quant Quickhand, and Short Simon dead, along with two of Jason Vasquez's cows."

"What?" Baron Sigrid's toga flopped as he reeled in shock. "Who did this?"

"Not 'who.' 'What.' A bearak." said Ian.

"Hah! Like as not you and Vasquez slaughtered my subjects and sought to blame Charles mythical monster."

Ian shook his head again. "These travelers were at the tree before my arrival." He gestured over his shoulder at the wagon. "I also ordered your serf's bodies transported to the old monastery."

"Huh! Better there than at the church here, I suppose." Baron Sigrid rubbed his head and winced, appearing drained. "Is there else I ought to know?"

Ian started to turn, paused. "Yes, Peter is back."

Baron Sigrid emitted a long sigh and rubbed his head. "Hopefully, he'll behave better this time. I do not want him on my lands." He retreated into the gate.

Ian mounted his steed. "My lady, if you'll have your man follow me, we should reach Cosslet keep well before sunset."

The cart rattled and bounced between a murky river west and dead fields everywhere else. Overhead, the leaden sky threatened to weep rain any minute.

Ian pointed out a blocky house surrounded by a tall stone hedge atop a nearby rise. "That's Jason Vasquez's farmstead." Ian spurred his steed and moved ahead of the cart.

Tia extended a finger into her pocket and touched the pouch within. *Just one hit. A little one. After today, I need it.* Her finger opened the packet and contacted the fine powder. Her pulse heightened with anticipation. The Blue Dust turned dreary days of travel into a cottony blur. Without it, she'd have gone mad, watching the scenery crawl past. She needed the Dust. It kept her sane.

She withdrew her finger. A fine bluish-purple particulate covered the last fraction of the digit. Enough for an hour. A year ago, this dose lasted a full day. *I am in control. I am not a wreck like Nyssa.* Tia shuddered as she remembered how Nyssa had degenerated from student to Dust addicted whore.

To hell with it. It's a small dose, only my second for the day. She brought the finger to her lips, and a sensation both sweet and salty exploded on her tongue. Shortly afterward, the dreary world around her became filled with subtle pastels and arcs of colors.

To Tia's eyes, Cosslet appeared as a surreal village of tidy pastel cottages wreathed in river mist with narrow lanes roamed by cloaked figures.

Perhaps being Baroness Cabbage wouldn't be so unbearable. Ian was cute, responsible, and caring. They'd make a good fit.

Thick streamers of fog looped around the moss-covered outer wall and solitary tower of Cosslet Castle, giving it the appearance of something from a fairy story.

Ian dismounted and approached the cart. "My lady, we've arrived at my ever so humble abode." He extended a tanned hand.

Tia suppressed a giggle and daintily offered her hand. Stepping from the wagon seemed an enormously complicated task; her foot somehow landed in the wrong spot, throwing her off balance and into Ian. Somehow, that seemed funny.

"My lady, are you alright?"

"I'm fine." Tia exhaled. "I'm just tangled."

"Ah, of course."

The keeps stout portal popped open like a giant cork. A thin man in a brown vest and wisps of white hair on his otherwise bald pate stepped into the yard. A stout woman in a stained apron over a once white dress stood next to him.

"My lord," said the man. "Did you apprehend the lawbreakers?"

"No, Bennet, I did not," replied Ian. "I did, however, spend time in the company of Baron Sigrid."

"With his hospitality, that means your plum famished," stated the woman. "I've got some stew on." She took stock of Tia. "You pick up some strays?"

"Ah," Ian faced the woman. "Marta, allow me to introduce Lady Tia Samos and her servants. Sir Peter was providing escort for her but became delayed by other business."

Ian's words penetrated Tia's mental fog like a sword stroke. "It was horrible! Those poor men!"

"What's this?" Bennet's face became a mask of hard angular lines.

Ian grimaced. "I'll explain once we're inside. I need to speak with Charles."

"Charles arrived here an hour ago, looking for you," said Bennet.

"Is he still here?"

"He's in your study."

Ian winced. "At least something went right today. We also need to get our guests settled for the evening."

"Of course, of course."

A retinue of servants appeared, one fat and stupid looking, one as old and weathered as a stone, and a third man who seemed made of long sticks draped in brown cloth.

Ian guided Tia into a tall, wide room and sat her in a comfortable overstuffed chair facing an intricate tapestry next to a crackling fireplace. The baron bowed. "My lady, I must address business."

Ian departed.

Tia found the tapestry wondrous. She lifted a finger, attempting to trace one of the lines. Shocked and outraged voices emanated from a great distance, breaking her concentration.

"My, you're a lovely one." The speaker stepped into Tia's view. He had curly red hair and a short beard set in a freckled face.

"Why thank you, good sir." Tia's cheeks warmed. The stranger looked cute.

The stranger extended a long muscular arm encased in a green cotton shirt. "I'm Charles, Baron Cortez's cousin."

A bell rang. "That's Marta, telling us dinner is served," said Charles. "Would you care to join us?"

Tia's cheeks went from warm to hot. "I'd be delighted."

Charles took Tia's hand and hoisted her from the chair.

The motion disrupted the haze clinging to Tia's mind. "I should freshen up first."

A smile appeared on Charles' lips. "Certainly, my lady. Follow me."

Tia stood in a small room before a large bowl of water with a cracked mirror on the wall. The face that stared back at her was blue eyed, more angular than curved, framed by blond hair. She touched the liquid, flinching at the chill. The Dust's influence began to dissipate. "Ok, then." She splashed water on her face. The mental fuzziness evaporated like morning dew. Her rose colored traveling dress was surprisingly clean and even mostly dry. Tia lifted a limp golden lock and let it drop. *My curls are a lost cause.*

"Permit me." Rebecca materialized alongside Tia. "Hm. I can't do much." The maid tapped her foot. "But that shouldn't matter."

Indignation rose in Tia's throat. "My hair's a mess. It's not acceptable."

"These are country folk." Rebecca produced a brush and ran it through Tia's hair. "They value substance over style. I'll make you presentable, never fear."

Tia considered Rebecca's words. Baron Ian didn't seem one to stand on ceremony. "Very well, then. I prefer glamorous, but presentable will suffice."

Tia entered the Great Hall with her hair tied in a single tail. Without the Dust's influence, the castle appeared more worn than wondrous. The previously exotic tapestries now looked faded and moth-eaten. Light patches on the walls showed where curios had once hung.

Two tables dominated the chambers end. Baron Cortez, Benet, and a black-robed priest sat at the closer one; Kyle and the castle servants lined the other.

"Allow me." Charles materialized next to Tia and slid a black wooden chair with a pink seat cushion.

Tia smiled and ignored the cracked armrest. "Why, thank you." She sat and contemplated the faded tablecloth, set with smoky glass cups, tan ceramic bowls, and chipped plates.

Tia watched the plump woman in a stained dress filled the glasses from a green bottle. *Wine today. But ale most others, I wager.*

Tia examined the cutlery. Wooden spoons and iron eating knives instead of proper silver. Peasant implements. Old stains dotted the napkins. Scratches marred the unadorned plates and bowls. Her cup was chipped.

Baron Ian took a sip from his glass and exchanged words with the Steward. Then he turned his attention to Tia. "My dear, what business brings you to my humble adobe?"

Direct and to the point. Good. I can't do 'subtle' right now. Tia put on her warmest expression. "I locate potential business opportunities for the master merchant Palo Rubinus. He feels many entrepreneurs in the empire could benefit from an influx of capital." She didn't mention the prospective betrothal. Too soon. Besides, the Baron already knew.

Ian's brows furrowed. "Most people hereabouts are farmers. Still, before the Occupation, Cosslet, Caestoninus, and Lupton boast a dozen prosperous enterprises ranging from mines to woodworks." He sighed. "Those days are past. Still, there are two or three artisans whom you might approach. Master Anatoly in Lupton is an expert woodworker whose pieces sell as far away as Xenon, and Master Nickolas in my fief produces superb wool cloth."

Tia nodded. Both craftsmen were on her list of prospective clients.

The priest regarded Tia over intertwined fingers. "Lady Samos, I am Father Barnabas, prelate of Saint Andrews here in Cosslet. Will your business keep you in our fair village past tomorrow?"

"It might." A chill entered Tia's bones. The priest referred to the Autumn Equinox, known across the Empire as Hell Day. Fell spirits stalked the land, minds became inflamed with spite, and devilish omens appeared in the sky. Sane folk spent Hell Day in church mouthing prayers.

"Ah, might I invite you to seek sanctuary at Saint Andrew's?" The priest leaned toward her. "'Tis most comfortable, and no unclean spirit has breached its walls."

"I shall, if my business keeps me here." Given Cosslet's poverty, that seemed unlikely.

Marta appeared with a platter heaped with bread. Behind her, two boys lugged a caldron. She sat the loaves in the table's center while the boys ladled generous amounts of vegetable stew into the bowls.

Tia raised the laden spoon to her lips. "Delicious." She meant it.

"Marta is a superb chef," said Ian.

"Our repast is plain," said the Baron as if reading Tia's mind. "Once we grew three kinds of grain and boasted orchards of apples and pears, stands of green spice and other crops as well. Since the Occupation, we are reduced to one species of grain, potatoes, and piles of cabbages." He winced. "Count yourself fortunate cabbage is not on the menu tonight."

"I'm certain your expert management will make Cosslet bloom again," said Tia.

Ian exhaled. "Thank you, My Lady. I expect to add apples and green spice to the menu next year."

The stick-thin servant approached Baron Cortez and bowed. "My lord, Sir Peter has arrived."

Peter appeared with his hair neatly combed, face scrubbed, and his torso encased in a maroon shirt. He claimed the tables last vacancy.

"We found three more cows, two living, one dead. The bearak's trail vanished into the brush."

"It escaped."

"It did." Peter took a mouthful of stew. "We took the peasants bodies to the monastery, but found it deserted."

"Deserted?" Father Barnabas leaned across the table. "How odd. Where did you leave the remains?"

"We found a cellar," said Peter around a mouthful of bread. "But the bearak must be found."

"Bearak's can be hard to find," said Charles.

Bennet glared at Charles. "This one certainly eluded you long enough. Just like that werewolf last year."

Charles made to rise. "Curb your tongue! I killed that shifter and I'll kill this beast!"

Peter stirred at the exchange. Werewolves were another bugaboo of the Kirkwood. Rumors claimed the army recruited wolf-men as infiltrators during the war, but that hadn't worked out – they were too unbalanced, prone to attack anybody, not just the enemy.

Tia's head started to pound. *What is it with men and fighting? Didn't they get their fill of slaughter in the war?*

Ian pounded the table. "I intend to slay this beast tomorrow and hang its pelt above my mantle."

Benet's face colored. "My lord, to risk yourself is irresponsible!"

Ian faced the steward. "My office demands I protect Cosslet's inhabitants. Ignoring the bearak's depredations is irresponsible. Besides, I won't be alone. Guardsman Carter is a stout fellow."

"I can track the beast." Charles glared at Benet, "Just like I tracked that werewolf to its lair and put an arrow through its heart."

"Go for it." A grim smile fixed itself on Peter's face. "I shall accompany you. Arrows are the best way to kill a bearak, and we have arrows aplenty."

"Three men are not enough," said Bennet.

The baron stroked his chin. "I am confident Jason Vasquez will join our expedition. And Alex Rodriguez. With my man Carter, that brings our number to seven." Ian faced Charles. "Perhaps you could spare a half a dozen woodsmen? They are a doughty lot."

Charles shook his head. "They are deep in the Kirkwood." He leaned back in his chair. "Seven well-armed men are sufficient to dispatch the bearak."

Tia pushed aside her plate. "Well, while you stalk this monster, I shall stalk investments."

"No," said Sir Peter. "I insist you remain here until the bearak is dispatched."

"I concur," said Charles.

Tia fought to keep her features impassive. *Damn him! I cannot have my authority questioned.*

Sir Peter shook his head. "I am employed by Master Rubinus as your guardian. The beast is too dangerous for you to be abroad alone."

"I won't be alone." Tia smiled. "Kyle shall accompany me."

Kyle's head jerked erect.

The Baron frowned. "Master Nikolas's establishment is close at hand. And the inn lays an excellent table. The bearak is hardly likely to rampage through town."

"Thank you, Baron Cortez." Tia inclined her head.

Peter raised his hand. "My lady, this is most unwise."

Charles scraped his chair back. "Lady Tia, I suggest you heed your guardian. This beast is dangerous in the extreme."

Images of the mangled corpses at the Boundary Tree flashed into Tia's mind. "I – I shall consider your words."

Charles placed his hands on the table. "Lady Samos, I strongly suggest you obey, not merely consider."

Ian and Peter both glared at Charles. Marta stared at her plate. A tense silence filled the room.

"How about a tune?" A few chords accompanied Rebecca's words.

Ian smiled. "We have not had a decent singer here in ages."

Rebecca bowed and launched off into the 'Shepherd and the Serving Girl.' Charles smiled. Marta blushed at the bawdy bits. Tia relaxed.

Rebecca followed that song with the more refined 'Summer Breeze' which morphed into 'Daisy Lane.'

Tia yawned. "I find myself fatigued from today's exertions."

The Baron nodded. "Of course, Lady Tia. Marta will show you to the guest suite."

Marta began climbing the spiral staircase at the back of the hall. "This way, dearie."

Tia followed the plump woman. *God above, I need another hit.*

The plump cook guided Tia to a chamber that boasted a large bed covered with a colorful quilt and little else.

Marta pointed at Tia's trunk, placed in the room's corner. "Your servant brought that in earlier." Faint disapproval underscored the cook's words.

Heat rose in Tia's cheeks. "That was good of him."

"He's a strong one." Marta left without a word.

Tia flopped on the bed. It felt soft. Wondrous. Images warred in her head. Dead bodies and dying towns. A Baron who chased cows and ate no better than his servants. Responsible, but no doubt drowning in debt.

A knock sounded at the door. "Enter."

Rebecca came inside and sat on the bed beside Tia. "Well?"

"Well, what?"

"Are you visiting the local merchant's tomorrow?"

"Oh, that." Tia brought a hand to her chin. "Probably. Maybe. I don't know." She turned her head. "Why? Do you have plans?"

"I might." A mischievous smirk appeared on Rebecca's face.

Tia smiled. "Would those plans involve a certain handsome huntsman?"

Rebecca's smirk intensified. "None of your business."

"Charles is cute, though."

"I don't know," said Rebecca. "Charles is a charmer, but he's got hard edges. But he's not your concern. Baron Cortez is."

EMPIRE: COUNTRY IV - Peter

Peter watched Marta guide Tia to the top of the staircase, still wobbly from the Dust.

Drinkers and drug takers had filled the war camps. Peter knew too well the fumbled speech and bouts of weariness of habitual Dusters. He'd taken to the drug a few times himself after Tessa's death. But he hadn't let the substance rule him.

Tia looked so much like Tessa. *I failed to save Tessa. I will protect Tia.*

Behind Peter, Charles cleared his throat. "Well, if we're hunting bearak tomorrow, then I have a bear of a task ahead of me tonight."

Peter turned away from the stair. "I will see you at dawn." Charles tromped to the door, trailed by the priest.

"We need to talk." Ian walked towards the stairs.

"Certainly."

Two turns brought them to the upper floor. A short passageway brought them to the Baron's study. Ian opened the door with an iron key.

Inside, half-empty shelves gathered dust on the right wall, across from a map of Cosslet, Lupton, and Caestoninus baronies. Ian's desk and a set of overstuffed chairs dominated the intermediate space.

A pair of pictures alongside the entry caught Peter's eye. The first showed Cosslet Castle wreathed in green vines. The other depicted Ian and a dark-haired woman Peter didn't recognize. "These are of decent quality."

"Celina's work." Ian sounded distracted. "She's talented with a brush."

"Celina wasn't at the table tonight." Peter picked out familiar faces in the first picture. Ian stood atop the battlements, Bennet at his side. Marta's lumpy features peeped from the kitchen window.

"She's at her cousin's house." Ian's voice assumed a tone of business.

Peter turned away from the painting.

"Lady Tia appeared scattered this afternoon. Tell me, is she truly a mercantile agent?"

Peter stiffened. "Lady Tia does possess issues, but she is a registered agent of master merchant Palo Rubinus."

"Thank goodness." Ian's voice held a note of mock relief. "I'd feared she was merely yet another wealthy commoner's daughter seeking a husband from the aristocracy."

Peter curled his lips into a grin. "Tia's parents do regard her marriage as their pathway to aristocratic rank. We departed Xenon two months' past with a list of four candidates. Tia deemed the first three unacceptable."

"How did I make the list?"

"I added your name," Peter spoke in a deadpan voice.

"You shouldn't have."

Peter regarded Ian. "Other prospective brides have called here?"

"Two in the past year." Ian motioned at the portrait. "Calista White, from Nomos, my three-week fiancé. She adored me, despaired at the climate, and her parents balked at my debts. I'm not altogether disappointed. A wrongness clung to Calista." He flopped back in the chair. "Celina liked her, though. Nadine came after her, took one look at my glorious realm, and fled. And now you bring me another status seeker."

"Yet you didn't turn Tia away."

"That would be inhospitable." Ian slumped in his seat. "Besides, I need a nice fat dowry. Coppers trickle in, and silver bleeds out."

"How bad is it? Is that coin-counting pig still purchasing the Caestoninus lands with your coin?"

Ian waved a hand. "Oh, I am current with Master Brutus." The Equitant merchant bought the neighboring districts uninhabited remanent two years ago along with its attendant debts. He collected on the later to pay for the former. "His hairy minion Gunther visits every month to collect his pound of flesh." Ian leaned back in his chair. "Last time I had to sell Aunt Agatha's wardrobe to satisfy the scoundrel. Next time I may offer a cartload of cabbages. Give them somewhat to eat in that filthy warehouse of theirs."

Peter winced. "The bastards denied us shelter today."

"They deny everybody shelter." Ian straightened. "Quite inhospitable. I have fielded a dozen complaints about their behavior, but that warehouse squats on Master Brutus's land, not mine."

"What of Sigrid?"

Ian winced. "Our arrangement holds. Barely."

Peter scowled. "That arrangement will cost you Cosslet. How can Celina stand that twit?"

"Liam's not a bad sort," said Ian. "But Sigrid isn't the problem."

"Then who is?"

"Proconsul Rutherford." Ian tugged at drawer beneath the desk.

"What? The imperial governor?" The provinces consuls and barons answered to Rutherford, who'd been made governor after the massacre of the Cato family during the war.

"You heard me. Now, where did I put that?" Ian heaved a pile of ledgers and papers onto the desk. "Bella kept these books far better organized than I do." A shadow of old pain flashed across Ian's face. Fever claimed Ian's wife after the war. "Ah, here we are." Ian slid a parchment across the desk.

Peter leaned over the paper, noting the ornate seal from the governor's office at its bottom. He began reading the document. "Foundation in poor condition...a mandatory evacuation of premises if repairs not completed...one year to comply? Ian, I'd thought you'd convinced Rutherford to space the repairs out. Did you appeal?"

"I dispatched an appeal straightaway. The Proconsul's response ordered me to 'comply or face penalties.' I then ventured to Cato to plea in person. Rutherford's weasel of a clerk denied my audience."

"This sounds dodgy."

"It is dodgy." Ian rummaged beneath the desk and extracted another sheaf. "I obtained this estimate from the master builders 'Atlas and Klein.' They wanted seven thousand dinars for a 'full restoration,' and two thousand just to repair the foundation and cracked walls. When offered the stone from the east wing in payment, they dropped their bid to six and one, respectively. I don't have six thousand dinars. Hell, I don't have sixty dinars, not with the war taxes and debts. If I don't do something, I'll be a homeless vagabond!" He gave Peter a pleading look. "Will Tia grant me a loan?"

Peter let out a long breath. He'd dreaded this moment. "I can ask." His tone gave Tia's probable answer

"A low-born merchant would dare to refuse a loan to their betters?"

"The mercantile lords of Equitant did not become wealthy through foolhardy investments."

"Well then, I may have to marry her." Ian shoved the papers back in the drawer.

"I can help you with that." There. He'd said it.

Months of scheming flashed through his mind.

Tia. In her, Peter saw salvation for himself and the Cortez clan. Pretty. Rich. Connections that spanned the empire. And a spitting image of Tessa. No, don't think about that. Tessa was gone.

Tia's family were wealthy commoners. They sought the privileges and status of the aristocracy and saw marriage as the means to that end. Specifically, Tia's marriage. They even had a list of prospective candidates and mapped out a jagged route to each in turn.

At first, playing escort had been a job, an honorable means of earning coin. Watch the road. Ignore her laugh – so much like Tessa's.

The Bottle's had been first, specifically Lord Caspar Bottle, a young rake who'd gleefully wined and dined Tia, introducing her into his circle of decadents. He meant her no good – Peter knew Caspar's ilk from the War Camps – overblown aristocrats who used and abused one woman after another. The thought of Tia – so very much like Tessa! – Being abused and discarded rankled Peter. That Caspar intrigued Tia was even worse. Peter couldn't help himself. He approached Rebecca, had her strum a warning tune – and Tia took the hint. They left the Bottle Estate with no commitments beyond a wine contract.

Next, they'd gone to Forest Bridge, just inside the Kirkwood, to call upon Lord Issyk Cassidy in his brooding gray keep above the Lona River. That worthy's gravestone pallor and hollow voice counted against him straight away. Still, he displayed courteous manners in their initial encounter, waxing eloquent on his clan's lengthy history. Tia's polite interest resulted in an excruciating tour of Lord Cassidy's family crypts and a swift departure.

'Fallen men marry low.' Tia made that comment to Rebecca, but Peter had been nearby, and heard every word. Those words started him thinking. He remembered Ian and promises made in the past. Ian was twice the man than rakish Caspar or dour Cassidy. More, their zig-zag route would take them right past Cosslet Barony.

Fortunately, Sir Richard Osmic's gluttonous bulk outweighed his pleasant demeanor and concern for his subjects in Tia's eyes. He'd been more concerned about a conflagration left half a village a charred ruin rather than courting Tia. Their stay at his quiet hall had been perfunctory.

That was when Peter had approached her about Ian, extolling his half-brother's status (a Baron, not a mere Lord!) and virtues – young, charming, industrious, set just a hop, skip, and a jump from Osmic's domain.

With but one other name left on her list, Tia reluctantly agreed to the detour. And here they were.

Ian regarded Peter. "I sense a demand, brother."

"You sense correctly." Peter steeled himself. "I want my name. Full legitimacy. An estate. And a position. Sheriff. I want to come home again. I'm tired of being a wandering hedge knight, no better than a mercenary."

"That's quite a list," said Ian.

"Tia's coin is your salvation. She can say 'no.' But I can persuade her otherwise." He hoped.

"Full legitimacy." Ian tapped the desk. "That requires approval by the Church and Emperor."

Peter formed his lips into a grim smile. "The request must come from the family's patriarch." He jabbed a finger at the Baron. "That's you."

"I sent off letters after your last visit," said Ian. "But turtles move faster than the bureaucracy." He tapped the desk again. "I can renew those requests."

"Do so."

"Groveton," said Ian. "It's abandoned now, but I intend to have it resettled. You're about the closest there is to a proper heir. Does that suit you?"

An empty home for an empty man, Peter thought. Also, about as far away from Lupton as he could get and still be in the barony. "It will suffice." He'd have to find servants and a suitable squire. Perhaps he could interest Kyle in a position.

"Sheriff," said Ian. "Making you Sheriff would curl Sigrid's hairs right up."

Peter allowed a smirk on his face. "Nothing wrong with that."

"There is more to being Sheriff than busting heads, you know. Laws, taxes, that sort of thing."

"I'll learn." How hard could it be?

Ian stared at him. Then he nodded. "Then we agree. Are you sure she'll agree?"

"There are no certainties." Peter watched Ian's face fall. "But I can persuade her."

"For both our sakes, I pray you can."

A wave of weariness settled over Peter. He yawned and stretched. "I must sleep." He turned for the door.

"Wait a moment." Ian stood.

"What?"

"Peter, I want a straight answer. Are you confident this beast is a bearak?"

"Of course, it's a bearak." Peter's voice held a hard edge. *It must be a bearak.*

Old habit, ingrained in childhood, took Peter to the door of his old room, where he nearly collided with old Rufus and stout Willow on their way out, the former lugging a large bundle of cloth.

The servants stood to the side as Peter entered. "We swept, lit a fire, and brought in some blankets," said Rufus. The old servant's face resembled a raisin.

Peter gave them an absent glance. "I'm much obliged. Isn't this usually Ben's job?"

The lines on Rufus's face drooped. "Lung fever took Ben last year, my lord. Just Simon, Carter, and me for the heavy lifting these days."

Peter wondered how much 'heavy lifting' Rufus was capable of anymore. The old coot was well past fifty. "That sounds exhausting." *Cosslet Castle is not merely half ruined, but more than half empty as well.*

Rufus smiled. "Oh, I still manage a song and a card game most nights. But other days, I'm worn right to the bone."

Peter almost smiled. Rufus couldn't carry a tune with a wheelbarrow. But that didn't keep him from exercising his pipes.

Peter's childhood bed bore its old, checkered coverlet, the same worn red carpet covered the floor, and the chest against the wall matched his childhood memories. Blank spots marked the former locations of his wardrobe and armor rack. And the curtain was blue, not red. He shivered. The room felt both familiar and alien.

Peter sat on the bed and contemplated the two tiny tongues of flame at either end of a split log stuffed into the soot-blackened fireplace. Dark spots dotted the faded rug. *Ian needs to hire chimney sweeps. Comes from burning plain wood instead of fumar.* Fumar logs burned clean and hot. The sap from a single tree could heat a peasant's hut for a year. Smiths used fumar pulp to smelt metal. But those days passed with the Traag War. Entire forests of fumar trees perished to forge the armor and weapons for Solaria's legions. Now, fumar logs were worth their weight in gold – or at least copper. So now gentry and commoners alike burned wood.

Tia - so much like Tessa.

Tessa restored my humanity.

Peter reflected on that thought. Years of killing made him sick to the soul. Life didn't matter, not his, not anybody's. He'd been a creature of animal lusts, living to drink and fuck and kill, knowing that his own demise awaited at the hand of some other murderer. He regarded himself as a damned soul destined for Hell. Yet, others disagreed. An old knight renown for his wise council told him to 'Do good.' And then there was Tessa.

Tessa...

The fire crackled and popped. Peter removed his clothes and crawled beneath the covers.

"GET UP." A HARD OBJECT slammed into Peter's bicep.

Peter opened his eyes. Sir Benedict DuPauls hawkish face loomed overhead.

"The engineers and skirmishers have cleared a route to the passes summit. His Supremacy intends to fight." Sir Benedicts features blurred in and out of the shadows.

"Here?" A chill ran through Peter's bones that had naught to do with his fever. "Traag's whole damn army is perched on the ridge above us."

"That's why the emperor has ordered every knight to the mustering ground. Even sick sluggards like you." Sir Benedict jabbed Peter's arm with his gauntlet. "We are charged with breaking the enemy lines for his Supremacies Legions. Now, on your feet."

Peter stood. His legs wobbled. "My horse"-

"We dined on your horse yesterday." Sir Benedict thrust a grieve at Peter. "Here. Strap on your armor."

Cold lines ran through Peters limbs and sapped his strength as he accepted the curved bit of metal. A black stain marred one side. "I feel like shit." He emphasized the statement with a cough.

"A mere sniffle." Sir Benedict shoved Peter towards the tent flap. "Fresh air will speed your recovery. Now don your armor."

Peter shrugged into his leather gambeson. Portions of it were frayed. A long slash cut through the side. The garment needed repair. But that was squires work, and Peters last squire, the kid with the freckled face lay buried at Rat Lake.

Sir Benedict helped Peter strap on the breastplate and leggings. These, too, showed dents, stains, and punctures. Sir Benedict's armor was in no better condition. Exhausted and short on rations, the Solarian army stood on the brink of collapse.

Peter stared at the triangle of gray light framed by the tent flap. "I need a horse."

"Yes, you do." Sir Benedict thrust a small pouch at Peter. "Thirty dinars. Rumor says a warhorse is for sale in the Tail."

Madness. Finding a battle trained steed in the Tail was about as likely as finding a virgin in a whorehouse. And thirty dinar was nowhere near *enough to buy such a beast even if it existed. "You expect me to ride into battle on a plow horse?"*

"You'll ride into battle on a damn mule if I say so. Fight or be named Craven." Sir Benedict's words could chip steel. "Make it quick." He shoved Peter towards the light.

Peter staggered into the light and blinked. He stood in a muddy lane. Close-packed stained rectangular tents dominated the streets far side – the Sixth's Legions bivouac. Behind him rose the once colorful pavilions of the Optimus, temporary home to ten thousand imperial knights along with their squires, servants, and consorts. Both comprised a district of Marcher Camp, a mobile city with a six-digit populace.

Five legionaries tossed dice across the lane from Peter. Past them, another soldier sat in the mud and stared into space.

The Tail – the human trash that accompanied Solaria's army without being part of it. Whores. Dust peddlers. Thieves. Scavengers. And dealers in horseflesh. Peter stumbled along the lane. Centurions barked orders. Legionaries donned battered armor and eyed nicked blades.

The tiny legion tents gave way to large canopies adorned with the snake and staff sigil of Saint Aesculapius, patron of healers and herbalists.

Peter caught a flash of blond hair outside the nearest of these tents. "Tessa!"

The blond head spun in his direction. Pert blue eyes widened. "Peter! You should be abed."

"Sir Benedict say's I'm to fight," said Peter as Tessa wrapped her arms around him.

A scowl crossed Tessa's face. "That man's a monster. Tell him 'No.' You can hardly stand, let alone fight."

"I tried. It didn't work."

A Healer stepped from the tent and called Tessa's name. "I must leave. Don't get killed." Tessa released her grip and slid into the tent.

Peter took a deep breath. Moisture leaked from his eyes. I will marry her after the war. Assuming I survive this battle. Then he straightened his carriage and strode towards a large gate in an earthen wall lined with catapults. Ruts filled with muddy water turned the lane into an obstacle course. Peter sighed and selected a route next to a stack of barrels alongside the nearest catapult.

"Get away from those." A bushy-bearded engineer popped up from behind the canisters. Another engineer stood behind the first, fingering a crossbow.

Peter ignored the speaker. Insolent commoners. You'd think those wretched casks were their firstborn children.

Peter reached the portal as a pair of Centurions prodded a line of pale-faced and bleary-eyed troops though in the opposite direction. They look worse than I feel. The column passed. Peter stepped through the gate and into the Tail.

Mismatched shanties and tents rose around Peter. Gambling pits. Whorehouses. Peddlers. A Centurion dragged three soldiers from one establishment. A black-haired woman lay sprawled near another tent, half out of her skirt.

Peter paid these sights no heed, and instead strode to a crude paddock at the encampments edge. A solitary black horse gave Peter the evil eye from the enclosures center.

"You here to buy?" Brown eyes peered at Peter through a stringy mop of brown hair. Black spots covered the youthful speaker's teeth.

"Maybe." By some miracle, the kid had found a warhorse. It sported a coat black as sable crisscrossed with hundreds of purple scars. The horse lacked half its right ear and walked with a limp. Hard used. Like every other horse in the army.

"No maybe about it." The kid spat a brown glob into the dirt. "You got the money, or you don't."

"How much?" Malevolence radiated from the horse and gave Peter an uneasy sensation. It went unsold for a good reason. But a knight without a mount wasn't a knight.

"What yah got?"

"*Thirty dinars.*"

The kid snorted. "Not enough."

"*It's what I have.*" *I need a horse. Peter reached for his sword.* "*Coin or steel, your choice.*"

A heavy weight slammed into Peters side and knocked him into the mud.

"*I got eighty dinars.*"

Peter craned his neck and spied a face dominated by a blond mustache. Sir Walter Travis.

A broad grin split the youths face. "*Done.*"

Sir Travis pressed a pouch into the seller's palm and started for the paddock.

"*No.*" *Peter staggered to his feet.* "*That's my horse.*"

Sir Travis paused long enough to face Peter. "*Not anymore.*"

Peter reached for his sword.

A hard object pricked into Peter's lower back. "*My brother said, 'not enough.' The deals done. Sheathe that steel, Sir Pauper.*"

Peter released his grip and moved sideways. A second grubby youth stood behind him, hands wrapped around a crossbow with a cracked stock.

Peter slipped, lost his balance, and fell against the fence.

"*Pathetic, Sir Pauper. You can barely stand, let alone ride.*"

The strength fled from Peter and a chill soaked into his limbs. He's right. The world dimmed into a gray blur.

Bugles and a kinked neck woke Peter from his torpor. Pain flashed along his spine as he rolled his head and blinked. Columns of soldiers and phalanxes of knights poured from Marcher Camp's gates amidst a cacophony of drums and marching chants.

"*Loose!*" *The single word, repeated by multiple throats, carried above the din. A fusillade of shafts and stones flew skyward at the command, accompanied by a cloud of crossbow bolts and arrows. The majority struck the enemy line at just two or three points, obliterating the enemy racks.*

One pennant caught Peter's eye: a gold crown set in a blue field. "God above, the Emperor himself is taking the field." He took note of their path. God above, he's going to lead a charge straight up the slope. If the tactic worked, the enemy ranks would be split in twain. If the charge faltered, though, the knights would be massacred.

I should be out there. He struggled to his feet and managed two wobbly steps. Then he halted. I'm a knight without a steed. There's no place for me. He caught a glimpse of the Healers tents beyond the gate. Tessa. I can protect her.

Peter reached the gate as more bugles blared. The imperial standard ascended the hill, flanked by thousands of cavaliers.

And Traag's army responded. Companies of enemy knights poured down the hill, accompanied by regiments of men and packs of orange skinned hobgoblins, all converging on the emperor's standard.

Solaria's knights slammed into Traag's forces. Blood spurted. A song of pain and hate filled the air as dying screams mingled with the clash of steel and shouted commands. Traag's troops did most of the dying. But Traag's soldiers outnumbered Solaria's.

A fresh wave of Traagian troops descended the ridge. Solaria's cavaliers faltered, exhausted from their uphill charge and previous strife. Mobs of footmen surrounded and isolated the mounted champions. Acres of gray-clad enemy soldiers converged upon the knot of warriors with the imperial standard at its center. Arrows fell on the enemy like rain, but no larger missiles.

They'll be massacred! Where are the legions? He couldn't see a damn thing. Desperate, Peter clambered atop a broken cart and shaded his eyes. There. Ranks of disciplined legionaries ascended the hill in an unbroken line, flanking the enemy. But that didn't help the Knights. Or the Emperor. What's going on?

A black and red standard appeared on the ridge crest, next to a massive figure in black armor. True God above, that's him. The Warlord. One of Traag's Three. The Three: Traag's demonic rulers, steeped in evil

sorcery. That bastards black magic could lay waste to an entire legion –
he'd done so in the past.

Signal flags dipped. Engineers shouted commands. Then the catapult
arms moved, and dark objects arced towards the conflagration.

Peter eyed the missiles with professional detachment. Not enough.
And too scattered. Flame and thunderclaps filled the air. Peter's ears rang.
What deviltry is this?

A giant invisible hand swatted Peter from his perch. The sky flashed
overhead, and then his back exploded in pain. He couldn't breathe. Red
pain replaced thought. Reflex alone got Peter off his back. He gulped air,
but it wasn't enough. He swung a gauntleted hand at the wagon bed
and missed. His limbs seemed disconnected. The second time his hand
connected. He heaved himself to his feet.

Scrap wood and cloth from demolished shanties littered the street.
Screams made a chorus straight from hell. Dazed men and women
clambered from the wreckage. If it's this bad here, then what's it like on the
slope? He couldn't see the battlefield even with half the shacks leveled.

Cheers and shouts rang from the wall. "Ho! That got them!"

"To work, maggots. Give them another dose." Creaking sounds and
oaths reached Peters ears as the catapult arms dropped.

Those damn engineers did this.

Peter stumbled through the gate. Burly engineers lugged barrels to the
catapult pockets.

A massive guardsman stepped from the shadows, blade in hand. "Ho!
Who be you?"

"Sir Peter Cortez of Benedicts Bravo's, currently unhorsed." The words
emerged in a choked gasp that emptied his lungs.

"Knight, eh? You look like shit."

Peter took a great gulp of air and straightened his spine. "I can fight."

"Good." The guard's sword pointed at the parapet. "Up there with yah."

Each step sent fiery lines through Peter's limbs. His head cleared the
summit as the catapults cut loose a second time. Hundreds of barrels arced

towards the slope. Crap. Not again. Peter dropped as thunder roared a second time.

Explosive roars transformed into screams. Peter lifted his eyes. Smoke drifted across the battlefield and obscured his vision.

Peter mounted the walkway for a better view. Bodies carpeted the former location of Traag's center. The imperial pennant still stood. A pathetic handful of cavaliers climbed to their feet or tried to control their skittish horses. He didn't see Traag's Warlord. An enormous mob of enemy foot stampeded away from the devastation and into the line of imperial troops. The hardened legionaries slaughtered Traag's gray-clad minions in droves.

"Demon kissers is getting their asses kicked," said an engineer.

"Move your butts," shouted a voice near the catapults. "Get that arm cocked!"

More Traagian troops dropped from the ridgetop. Thousands charged the imperial banner. The remainder swarmed towards the embattled legions. But a large knot ignored both groups and headed straight for the camp.

"Demon kissers wised up," shouted the engineer beside Peter. He glanced at Peter's sword. "You good with that thing?"

Peter didn't deign to answer.

"Move, metal ass," said a voice from the stairs.

Peter stepped aside as a pair of large men heaved a barrel atop the parapet. A cold knot formed in his gut. "What are you doing?"

"Stopping them louts." The speaker pried a cork from the canisters end.

"Make haste, damn you," said the guard beside Peter. "They're almost here. Oh, shit, they got Spawn!"

Peter lifted his head. A solid wall of orange hobgoblins and warriors in black armor carved with runes raced through the tail. Spawn: once human soldiers infused with demonic magic, stronger and faster than mere mortals. Spawn didn't give up and didn't retreat. Instead, they obeyed their master's orders even if doing so claimed their lives. Peter had tangled with Spawn thrice before. He'd won twice. A fortuitous arrow saved him the third time.

"Got it," shouted the trooper alongside the barrel. "Go!"

The engineers heaved the barrel over the walls far side. It hit the ground, bounced, rolled, and slammed into a dilapidated shack mere yards from the nearest squad of Spawn.

"Down!"

Peter didn't need the reminder. He hit the parapets floor as orange light flared and an immense roar filled the world. Objects fell to the ground around him. One pinged off his back and landed next to his nose. It was a black metal glove with a severed hand inside.

Peter and the engineers rose to their feet. Not much remained of the Tail. Or of the attackers.

"We got them," said the soldier alongside Peter. Then he doubled over and grabbed at the black-feathered shaft in his gut.

A second shaft clattered off Peters armor and zinged into the encampment. Peter dropped. His eyes scanned the debris. There. Small green shapes darted among the wreckage. Goblins. Too puny for straight-up fights. Instead, they served as scouts and ambushers.

Other shapes rose from the ruins – hobgoblins and Spawn. They ran towards the wall.

Peter's companions produced crossbows. A dozen-odd enemies fell with shafts in their bellies or throats, but the rest didn't halt. Then they were atop the wall. A black-armored warrior with crazed eyes confronted Peter.

Steel collided with steel. Sparks flew, and blood flowed, and then Peter found himself splayed out on the street, the Spawn face-down beside him.

Melees raged along the parapet for control of the catapults. Goblins dropped from above and ran into the camp.

Screams reached Peter's ears from the tents of Saint Aesculapius. Tessa. Fear gave strength to Peter's limbs. He reached Tessa's tent just as a trio of goblins emerged. His blade swung again and again. And the screams didn't stop.

Then he knelt before a slight form in a blood-stained dress. Tessa. Tears poured from his eyes. He blinked. The corpse bore Tia's face.

EMPIRE: COUNTRY V - Tia

"Wake up sleepyhead," said a high-pitched voice from the region of Tia's feet, which seemed weighed down somehow. "Marta will be mad at you if you miss breakfast."

Tia opened her eyes. A round young female face fringed by dark curls peered at her from close range.

"And just who are you?" Tia freed one arm from beneath the sheets. "A little imp that lives in the walls?" She didn't want to leave her warm, comfortable nest.

"No silly, I'm Celina. Ian is my daddy." She assumed a position that was both dignified and comical, one that stretched her cream shift. "He's the baron."

"I thought that name sounded familiar," said Tia, giving the girl a little poke in the arm.

Celina giggled and jumped off the bed. "Hurry up and get downstairs," she said as she skipped towards the door. "You really don't want to make Marta mad."

Tia rubbed her eyes and climbed out of bed, stepping onto a well-worn but clean rug. She spied a washbasin in a niche off to one side, with a flagon of water next to it. Reaching the washbasin meant walking across the cold wood floor. She splashed water on her face and ran her fingers through her hair – there was no mirror. Where was Rebecca? Drat. She'd have to make herself ready. Tia spotted her trunk, opened it, and extracted a hand mirror, along with a bone-handled brush.

"Hurry up," piped Celina's voice through the door.

"Oh, there you are, you little monster – hounding the guests, are we?" Tia didn't recognize this new voice, but it was female, older, and sultry.

"I'm trying to get ready," she called.

"You can help her, aunty!" said Celina. "You're really good at that!"

"Celina, no!" Too late. Celina bounded into the chamber.

An attractive woman in her mid-twenties entered behind the girl. She boasted black hair in a style that only looked casual, gorgeous green eyes, and sufficient curves to have every male within miles howling at the moon. She wore a burgundy dress that only accented her features. "I'm sorry," she said, trying and failing to apprehend Celina, who skipped away, "but she does things like this all the time." She held out a hand with crimson fingernails. "I'm Vanessa, by the way, Baron Ian's cousin."

"Wow, is all this stuff yours?" Celina pawed through Tia's chest. "I bet you'd look good in this," pulling out a skimpy black dress that Tia had worn to less than refined social events back in Solace.

"Celina," that's not yours," said Vanessa, hands on her hips. "Go downstairs and wait for us."

Celina made a face and stuck out her tongue.

Vanessa tapped her foot and glared.

"I was just looking!"

Celina slid towards the door.

Vanessa turned to Tia. "Here, I'll comb your hair." Without further ado, she picked up a comb and began running it through Tia's long blond tresses.

"I don't remember you at dinner last night."

"That's because we were over at Lizzie's," piped up Celina who hadn't quite made it out of the room. "Lizzie is my best friend in the whole wide world."

"I told you to go downstairs, you little monster!"

"Lizzie?" asked Tia.

"Elizabeth Cortez, granddaughter of Henry Cortez, the Baron's uncle," explained Vanessa.

"It is kind of you to take her there."

"She just wanted to do icky things with Edward." Celina punctuated the statement by sticking out her tongue.

"Why, you little pest." Vanessa made a less than playful swipe at the child

"It's true," insisted Celina, "That's why we share a room here, so that she won't do icky things with boys."

Vanessa threw Tia's comb at the girl, who dodged, squealed, and ran out the door.

"I'm so sorry about that!"

"I have difficult younger sibling's myself."

Vanessa gave Tia's locks a dozen long strokes. "There – that must suffice."

Tia followed Vanessa to the stairs, illuminated solely by weak shafts of lights through tiny window slits.

Tia's shoe snagged on a hole in the worn carpet, pitching her sideways into a faded pastoral tapestry in an explosion of dust. The ancient cloth sunk into the wall as if it were the maw of a mythic beast and Tia its snack.

Tia felt a tug against her belt even as she raised a hand to brace herself. "Help me, Auntie!" said Celina's high-pitched voice.

Her hand sunk into the fabric and slid.

"Oh dear," said Vanessa.

Tia came to rest in a twisted heap in a nest of fabric sunk into the wall, with Celina atop her. She raised her head and glared at Vanessa. "What is this?"

"It's the wall," said Vanessa. "We're having some work done."

Celina wiggled free.

Tia struggled against the fabric but couldn't free herself.

"Liar! It's been like that forever!" Celina bounced on the stairs.

Vanessa extended a hand.

Tia let the other woman lift her from the nest.

"What sort of work?" Tia noticed a pale sliver of daylight between the edge of the tapestry and the wall. She shuddered as a draft of chilly air seeped in through the opening.

"Cosslet keep was damaged during the Occupation," said Vanessa.

"Yeah! We had ugly goblins and big smelly Scrotti men right outside the wall!" Celina pointed at the opening. "That's where a great big rock hit the castle. Daddy and Uncle Peter took their swords and chopped off their heads."

Vanessa glared at the girl. "You weren't even born yet, brat."

"Daddy told me all about it, so there!" Celina stuck her tongue out.

Tia cautiously pushed against the side of the tapestry, revealing a gouge in the building that dropped into a giant heap of rubble.

"That's the old east wing," said Vanessa.

"It got knocked down by three big stones," said Celina. "Wham! Wham! Wham! Then it fell. That was scary!" The little girl raised her hands, dropped them side by side and spread them apart. "Whoosh! Just like that."

"We better get downstairs before Marta gets angry." Vanessa stared at her feet.

After last night's supper, Tia had feared breakfast might be bread and porridge; but instead, it was eggs, bacon, and toast. Celina was right, though; Marta did seem visibly upset at her guest – Tia thought she heard a whispered 'lazy layabout' once. She had two eggs, a piece of ham, and a large piece of toast – more than the other two girls put together.

Afterward, she walked around the wall of the hall, idly noting the paintings and portraits that adorned it – as well as bright spaces on the walls where other items had been removed. *My host is reduced to selling family heirlooms to make ends meet.*

"I painted that one and that one," said Celina, pointing to images of her father and an older couple – presumably, Henry Cortez and his wife.

"You did?" It was customary for well-born children to be taught the basics of art, but most – including herself – were only barely proficient at such crafts. Celina, though, showed real talent.

"She did," said Vanessa. "The little demon is quite talented with a brush. She has a studio in our room."

Tia considered her options. Staring at mostly blank walls held little appeal. Dust? Her supply was almost exhausted. She turned to Vanessa. "Could you take me to the roof? I wish to view Baron Cortez's domain."

"Of course," said Vanessa.

"Let's go!" Celina dashed for the stairs.

Scaling the winding stair to the tower's summit left Tia with burning calves and shortness of breath. Vanessa appeared unaffected by the climb, and Celina if anything, seemed energized by the exertion.

Tia gazed at the castle below in dismay. Tumbled stones marked the location of the destroyed wing. The outer wall was nothing but rubble in two locations. The roof of a large outbuilding was caved in, as though smashed by a giant foot.

The brown bulk of the Stag River oozed southward mere yards from the moss-covered western wall. A narrow bridge arched across the stream to the castles south. From there, an arrow straight road vanished into the green wall of the Kirkwood.

Celina pointed at a log house at the forest's edge. "That's Cousin Charlie's place. He's the emperors Forester."

"Charles seems an interesting sort," said Tia.

"He's my cousin," said Vanessa. "He's also related to Sigrid on his mother's side."

Tia parsed this information. "So, he has a claim to both Cosslet and Lupton?"

Vanessa looked at her. "Well, yes, if about twenty people died."

Tia blushed and walked clockwise along the walkway. North, a faded road cut through a swath of farms.

"Groveton used to be that way," said Vanessa.

"The Scrotti killed everybody there." Celina made a face.

"Oh." Tia continued her walk. East, scrubland, and patchwork fields stretched towards a distant line of hills.

Vanessa motioned at the hills. "The Blight – land ruined by mine runoff – is past those hills."

"What of the mines?" Tia eyed the hills. "Are they on Ian's lands?"

"About half are," said Vanessa, "But they're worthless, played out even before the war. It's been years since anybody went and looked at them."

"Hm." Even played-out mines had their uses. Gravel, for example. Certain types of tailings were used to make dyes. A thought struck Tia – Brutus's wealth came from the manufacture of army uniforms, specifically their crimson cloaks. Was that what his agents were doing? Making dyes?

There was also another use for certain types of mine waste, one not commonly advertised. A use of particular interest to her parents. *I might have to inspect this 'Blight' in person.*

Cosslet town lay to the south: A triangular square lined with stone shops dominated the settlements northern side, with neat rows of round cottages to the south, the whole enclosed by a palisade of earth and logs.

From this height, the townsfolk appeared no bigger than dolls. But they seemed well groomed and dressed, at least from a distance. "Cosslet seems more prosperous than Lupton."

"Oh, it is." Vanessa pointed at a large stone building south of the town proper. "Master Nickolas is probably richer than Ian. He makes wool coats and cloaks." She pointed at another building across the square from Nickolas's, this one a walled compound. "Trevor's

Roadhouse is prosperous as well – it's the last good inn until you reach Ovid."

"That's where Silam will be holding his show!" Celina bounced around Tia. "You want to come? Will you take me?"

"Celina!"

Tia's smiled. "She's certainly direct." No doubt this 'Silam' was a wandering entertainer, unable to compete in the likes of Solace or Xenon. Third rate entertainment – another reason to cross this place off her list.

"She's spoiled rotten."

"I am not! You're the one always doing icky things with boys." Celina skipped along the edge of the wall.

Tia's gaze followed the road south to a collection of dark dots in the distance. "Is that Lupton?"

Vanessa nodded. "It's only six miles from here. Ian's lands extend to the town gates."

"The baron mentioned a Master Anatoly last night."

"He's making me a dollhouse!" Celina hopped across the roof. "With a little lady and a knight to protect her."

Tia considered the road again. In the broad light of day, it certainly seemed safe enough. She turned to Vanessa. "I believe I shall call upon Master Anatoly this morning."

"Can I come with you? Can I?" Celina was jumping up and down so fast she seemed to be vibrating. She turned to Vanessa. "You think he'll have my dollhouse done yet?"

Vanessa ignored the little girl. "Consul Sigrid won't care for that."

"Then I shall pay a call upon the good Consul."

"He'll likely keep you waiting till dusk, or have Kessler turn you away. He detests the new gentry."

Tia tapped her foot.

"He won't keep me away, though," said Celina.

Tia knelt and put her hands on the child's shoulders. "And why is that?"

"Cause' I'm getting married to his grandson Liam. I can see him anytime I want and bring anybody with me. It's part of the treaty."

Married at twelve. A tremor ran through Tia's body. That seemed young, even for the country. She looked at Vanessa. "Is this true?"

Celina spoke before Vanessa could answer. "Course it's true, silly. Everybody knows that."

"The betrothal takes place in three years," said Vanessa. "Sigrid forced Ian into it." She clearly didn't wish to discuss the matter further.

Married at fifteen. Better than betrothed at twelve. It still seemed young, though.

Celina hopped around the women. "Can I go? I'll be good."

"Oh, all right," said Vanessa. She turned to Tia "If it's alright with you, that is."

Tia considered. Traveling with a hyperactive girl held little appeal, but she needed access to Sigrid. "Yes, I believe you can accompany me."

"Yes!" Celina bounced across the room.

"Well, then," said Tia. "I shall have to see about making myself presentable. Tia frowned. She hadn't seen Rebecca anywhere this morning. "Where did that gypsy woman get off too?"

"Gypsy?" asked Vanessa.

"My maid Rebecca. She's a gypsy, quite skilled with cosmetics."

Vanessa pondered a moment. "I saw a gypsy woman leave the castle right before we entered. I thought she was part of the troupe."

"Troupe?"

"Yes, a whole pack of the wretches arrived day before yesterday, part of the entourage of the mighty Silam the Sorcerer." Vanessa's voice rang with mock enthusiasm. "His wagon was pulled by a droath! Imagine that!"

Gypsies. So that was where Rebecca was off to, no doubt hatching schemes with her wandering kin to swindle half the barony.

Tia felt a tug at her dress.

"Don't worry," said Celina. "Amelia can make you look really pretty."

"Amelia?"

"One of the servants," said Vanessa. "She is quite a good hairdresser."

Tia sighed and started for the door. "Well, if Rebecca has run off, then I must rely upon Amelia's services."

"I'll fetch her." Vanessa started for the door.

EMPIRE: COUNTRY VI - Kyle

Red pain shot through Kyles' leg as his foot pushed the pedal. The bicycle wheel turned, pushing him closer to the hilltop where a solitary tree overhung the track. Keep pushing the pedals. Then he'd be on level ground.

"This sucks." The new kid, Caleb. "Why are we out here, anyhow?"

"To kill pasties." Mack, short, solid, black-haired, and brutal.

"Shut it." Decurion Tug, squad leader, almost as big as Kyle. "Something moved."

"Huh?" Caleb faced Kyle with a quizzical expression on his face. Then something long and sinuous flopped over the kid's shoulder and wrapped itself around his neck. Caleb's face turned red. A choking sound emerged from his throat. Then he flew off the bike.

"Monster!" Diggers shout came from behind Kyle.

"Demon!" Mack.

Another tentacle lashed towards Kyle. He threw himself sideways. He winced as the ropy appendage missed his nose by about an inch. Then he was on the ground, tangled in a patch of yellow shrubbery, the bike frame pressing into his side.

"Argh!" Jasper writhed on the road, wrapped in tentacles, eyes bulging, futilely hacking at one with his short sword.

But it was the thing past Jasper that held Kyle's attention as he slithered backward, away from the bike. Big. Horse big. Six legs. And knife-like head framed by a writhing mass.

"Bearak." The thing sprouted a crossbow quarrel as Mack spoke the word.

The thing's knife head faced Mack.

Tug planted his short sword in the creature's backside.

It let out a godawful screech like a bird from hell. Two of its legs twitched.

Tug went flying. The thing was damn strong – the squad leader checked in at three hundred pounds with his kit.

Kyle extracted himself from the bike. He reached for his crossbow. Cocked it.

Another bolt sprouted in the things side while he loaded. It let out another godawful screech and dropped Jasper.

Mack hacked at a tentacle.

A tentacle quested towards Kyle's nose. He pulled the trigger –

- and woke, shaking and drenched in sweat.

DAMN. KYLE SAT AND rubbed his head. The nightmares just wouldn't stop. Booze dulled the pain, but that highborn bitch wouldn't let him drink. He winced, remembering the harsh 'crack' of the broken carriage axle. Drunkenness came with a hard price. At least he wasn't hung over.

Kyle closed his eyes and visualized a pinprick of blue light in a vast dark place. A deep hum emitted from his throat as he focused. The blue pinprick expanded, filling his head. Calm. Placidity. A cantrip so simple, so basic even he couldn't botch it.

He opened his eyes and took in the bedchamber, lit by dawns week light. Small. Cramped. Musty. Nothing but the bed, chest, and fireplace. A pair of crystalline pendants lay atop the chest. Had he correctly incanted the spell? He squinted and invoked his Sight. They emitted dull yellow gleams, invisible to normal vision.

Kyle frowned. He'd successfully imbued the trinkets, but the aura should have been green, not yellow. Strange. Had he made a mistake? Or were his powers fading from drink and disuse?

He shook his head. Finding was his chief strength as a sorcerer. The amulets alerted their wearers to the bearak's presence. *Or whatever that beast is.* The slime he'd extracted from the Boundary Tree yesterday didn't resemble blood. Or mucus. Or piss.

The massacre. Yesterday's nightmarish scene resurfaced. That slope. That tree. The dead bodies dangling from the branches – just like Caleb when they'd driven that Bearak off. For a moment, he hadn't been here, in Cato province, but there, in Barbaros. He repeated the cantrip of placidity. It took longer this time. His skin felt cold and clammy when he finished.

Well, that he could fix. Kyle stared at the half-burnt log in the fireplace. Focused. He imagined lingering the embers growing hotter, igniting. A tiny tongue of flame sprouted near the burned area.

Kyle was good with fire. Always had been. As a kid back on the Atticus estate, it'd been his duty to light the fires in the serfs quarters each morning. He could find embers hidden in scorched logs and cajole them into flame. All it took was focus and patience. Even cold ashes possessed hot spots that he could poke and prod and coax and reignite. He didn't think of it as magic – that was his sisters thing. Those two were forever poking through grandmothers books and trying this or that ritual, though never to any effect.

It was the same way with Fixing and Finding: fixing things, be it pitchforks, wagon wheels, or broken fences was part of a serfs life. His repairs went together and held up a bit better than others. His dad said it was because Kyle had a keen eye and a steady hand. Finding? Well, he was simply good at guessing, or remembering where something was at, or in the case of kids and animals, where they were likely to roam off to.

Kyle continued to think of those skills as 'knacks' right up until he caught the attention of a wizard in the Arcane Cohort. By then, he'd been in the legions for three years. That wizard – a gaunt, haunted man named Lysander – hauled him off to the military mage school at Mystic Mountain. There, he'd spent three long, frustrating years in towers and tunnels learning to turn his knacks into spells, along with a couple other tricks – most of which he could barely manage anymore.

Oh, Kyle had tried to better his arcane abilities since being discharged, going so far as to move to Solace and apply to its renown University, one of the empires great magical centers. There, he'd taken up with his old mentor Lysander, a disreputable archimage hounded by accusations of black magic.

Stories that circulated amongst the Universities students insisted Lysander used the forbidden magics of Jamison the Renegade during the war. Five centuries ago, Jamison's conjured demons halted one barbarian army in its tracks. Later, he'd employed mind bending sorcery to drive another horde into self-destructive fury. The clerics of Saint Ignatius rewarded Jamison by burning him at the stake.

The whole mess blew up when Lysander went to his daughter's wedding only to have the ceremony interrupted by witch hunters. Lysander fled the city, and Kyle ditched sorcery to take up driving Tia's carriage.

Enough. Kyle shrugged into his robe while the room warmed, and the log burned to a black core. He affixed strings to the crystals, making them into necklaces. The first he draped around his beefy neck. The second Kyle kept clenched in his palm and opened the door to the predawn gloom.

A figure emerged from the keep door. Peter. Kyle motioned him over.

"Here." Kyle dropped the talisman in Sir Peter's outreached hand. "Wear it under your tunic."

"What is it?"

"A means of warning. The glass becomes hot close to the bearak."

"How close and how hot?" Peter demanded. "This trinket won't set me alight, will it?"

Kyle shook his head. "The glass will grow warm within a stone's throw of the beast. It won't set anything on fire."

Peter gave the pendant a vertical toss and caught it again. "A stone's throw. Better than no warning, I suppose." The hand holding the amulet moved towards Kyle. "You'll be with Tia."

"I have one." Kyle pulled the second talisman from his robe.

Baron Cortez emerged from the keep, stretched, and yawned.

"I need to go," said the knight. "Keep Tia safe." Peter walked towards the stable.

"I will."

The two highborn rode from the stable a moment later accompanied by a leather-clad man at arms. A moment later they passed through the gate, and a large simpleton closed the stable door.

A stout peasant woman emerged from the dormitory. "Breakfast time. I'm Amelia, by the way." She didn't seem put off by the scar marring his face.

"Thank you. I'm Kyle."

"Oh, a polite one. Most men aren't so well mannered." Amelia turned and flounced into the keep.

Nobody sat at the highborn's polished slab, but Rebecca and a handful of menials occupied spots at the servant's table. Steam rose from a pot next to a bread platter.

Kyle peered into the cauldron and grinned at the sight of gruel dotted with diced apples. Good solid peasant's food. He claimed two bowls from a nearby stack, filled both, and handed one to Amelia. Then he grabbed two slabs of bread and sat. His smile broadened at the first bite. He emptied the bowl in short order.

Rebecca sat across from an old man, listening as he spoke between bites. "I must see for myself." Her colorful dress moved as she rose.

Kyle lifted his head. "See what for yourself?" Rebecca was a cipher to him. A gypsy servant? Yes, Tia was pleased with the girl. They gossiped and giggled and even sang together. But Kyle had known dogs with more sense than Tia. Everybody knew gypsies were thieves.

"Rovers," said Rebecca. "There's a troupe of them in town."

"Tia will want you when she wakes up." Kyle's voice held a note of warning.

Rebecca sauntered past Kyle. "Oh, don't worry. I'll return before Tia hauls her lazy ass out of bed." Then she was gone.

Kyle stood for a moment, then sat at the table. Rebecca had barely touched her porridge. *More for me.* He eyed the near empty flagon, wishing for more wine.

Marta popped from the kitchen and fumed that 'the tramp and the brat' were late again for breakfast and were no doubt tormenting the 'lady upstairs.'

So, he'd have to wait. That was nothing new. However, his pack held four or five of Tia's books. Polysperchon's 'Beasts of the World' might include an entry on bearak's.

Amelia followed Kyle to his chamber. Her eyes widened upon seeing the tomes.

Kyle didn't blame her. Books were scarce and expensive. He plucked Polysperchon's work from the heap, glanced at the rest, and handed Amelia 'Veritas's Geographica.' "You might like the pictures."

Amelia cradled the tome like a baby. "You can read?"

"Yes." Kyle wasn't surprised at her question. Only one peasant in four or five was literate.

They plopped down next to each other on the dormitory porch.

Kyle frowned. Polysperchon did write about bearak's, but the words were nonsense and picture was wrong.

Amelia giggled over her borrowed tome. She elbowed Kyle. "Do Saban's really dress like that?" She jabbed her index finger at a picture of an ebony girl clad in naught but a grass skirt and gold bracelets.

"I don't know," said Kyle. *Probably not if Veritas took after Polysperchon.*

"I couldn't go around like that," said Amelia. "And I bet that grass skirt itches."

"They do."

Kyle lifted his eyes. The sultry voice originated with a skinny, black-haired highborn clad in wisp of a dress that threatened to blow away in a breeze.

"And how would you know, Vanessa?" Amelia closed the book. "You've never been to Saba. Or anywhere else except Kitrin and Drakkar."

A dark mote entered Kyle's thoughts at Amelia's statement. Those words meant the highborn had spent time in the war camps. Which meant she had no virtue and fewer morals.

Vanessa smiled. "I know people who traveled to Saba."

"Sailors and scoundrels, I'm sure." Amelia handed the book to Kyle.

"Lady Samos must be made presentable for her excursions today," said Vanessa, "and her maid has vanished. That leaves you."

"Oh, all right." Amelia stood and dusted off her dress. Then she followed Vanessa back into the castle.

Kyle sighed. From experience, he knew that making Tia 'presentable' could take half the morning. He fetched Ginger and Buttons from the dilapidated stable and hitched them to the rented wagon. Next, he entered the dormitory and donned the absurd 'uniform' Tia insisted he wear - tall black boots, fine gray pants, and a long blue jacket with a ridiculous double row of brass buttons down the front. Despite crude alterations for his massive frame, the wretched coat still didn't button properly. A blue and black billed cap completed the ensemble.

Tasks completed, Kyle returned to the courtyard and cast a critical eye over the castle's exterior. Architectural and engineering issues leaped at him: an off-kilter foundation, a wide vertical crack in the keep tower, and a wing reduced to rubble. *The army would order this castle demolished.*

That thought prompted another wince. More images of the Traag War threatened to leak into his consciousness.

"I'm ready to go now." Tia stood before him in a rectangular dress favored by the Eastern aristocracy. Her hair looked odd. Stacked somehow. Whatever. Vanessa and a highborn child trailed behind her.

Kyle bowed. "Of course, my lady." Were they all going with Tia?

The child pranced over to Kyle. "You sure are ugly, mister. What happened to your face?"

Kyles fingers automatically went to the vertical scar that bisected his left eye socket. Frantic images surfaced in his brain.

KYLE DRANK THE WINE of courage. Energy coursed through his frame as the bugles sounded. He felt invincible.

"Forward! Double time," bellowed the Centurion. "Keep your shields locked."

Kyle kept his rectangular shield raised as the line of legionaries charged the hobgoblins line. He felt invincible. Unstoppable.

The orange-skinned creatures raised round shields and hefted an assortment of maces and battleaxes. They showed no inclination to retreat.

"We'll get them!"

"Die, demon worshippers!"

Then the hobs locked shields and charged.

The two lines of troops collided. Hot pain exploded in Kyle's shield arm. He stared at an orange-faced, pig-snouted monster square in its beady red eyes. The creature snarled, dropped its shield, and raised a massive double-bladed ax.

Kyle's sword stabbed towards the hobs armored body even as the ax fell.

Sword hit armor. The hob screamed in pain and rage.

The ax dropped.

Kyle lifted his shield.

The hobs ax split the shield in twain, and then pain exploded in Kyle's skull.

"A MONSTER'S AX DID that."

"Did it hurt? Did you kill it?"

"Celina!" Vanessa darted forward and snagged the child. "Stop pestering him and get in the cart."

Celina faced Vanessa and stuck out her tongue.

Tia gave Kyle a critical glance. "Even dressed up, you still look like an oaf."

"Yes, my lady." What else was he supposed to say?

Amelia steered Celina over, trying to suppress a giggle.

Kyle sighed and heaved the child into the wagon.

Celina glared at him. "You're strong, mister."

Kyle smiled and assisted the other two women. Then he slumped in the driver's seat and repeated his mantra of calmness.

"Kyle, stop muttering and start driving."

He straightened his shoulders, flicked the reigns, and drove the cart from the castle.

The women started gossiping immediately.

The slutty highborn told Tia about her ex-husband, "...woke up, and there he was, just dead – talk about gross"-

Even the women were gossiping about dead bodies. Why couldn't they talk about babies or clothes instead of corpses? He didn't need this. He tuned out the racket.

They passed a pair of boys kicking a ball. The sight brought back pleasant memories for Kyle of a time when he'd played 'kick-the-ball' with his peers on the Atticus Estate, and later, in the army. The commons loved that game. Clubs, identified by their colors, sponsored teams throughout the larger cities.

"Jeremy!" The highborn child leaped right out of the wagon, snatched the sphere, and kicked it into the shrubbery.

Vanessa jumped after her and caught the brat before she ran into the undergrowth.

"Celina, you're a mess." Vanessa brushed dead grass and twigs from Celina's dress.

Kyle ignored the screeching. Instead, he concentrated on the road.

A tug on Kyle's sleeve interrupted his reverie. "You gotta turn here. Celina pointed to a shop constructed of worn gray stone, flanked by a line of neat cottages. "You sure don't listen very well. I bet you were a bad soldier. That's why you got hurt."

Kyle grimaced and pulled into the lot. Celina hopped from the cart. Tia and Vanessa dismounted in a proper civilized manner. Then they realized Celina had vanished.

"She has friends here," said Vanessa before the two women walked to the shop's entrance.

Kyle propped himself against the cart. Sheep cropped brown weeds in the distance, watched over by teenage shepherds. Machinery thrummed inside Master Nickolas's establishment. The racket increased when a large door opened, and two stout women tossed thick bundles into another wagon.

"You're right. He is ugly."

Kyle directed his gaze downward. Celina reappeared with a plump, well-dressed lad of ten or twelve.

"A monster split his face open in the war," said Celina. "I bet it hurt."

Kyle moved his mouth, but no sounds emerged. Horrific memories of pain and blood and death danced behind his eyes.

"Now, now, don't torment the man."

Kyle turned as the children vanished. Father Barnabas stood alongside the wagon.

Kyle inclined his neck. "Thank you, Father. The war"-

The priest made a dismissive motion. "Oh, I know full well the war's effects on men's minds. Many of my parishioners are veterans." He shook his head. "Terrible things stalk their dreams and haunt their days. Some seek refuge in a bottle. Others go mad." He stared straight at Kyle. "Those who suppress the memories fare worst. Talking about them helps."

Kyle's brain threatened to seize working. Talk about those horrors? Relive those nightmares? Stupid. But others had issued identical advice. Military doctors. The Masters at Solace had proffered similar words. And Lysander, head of Kyle's mystic circle. 'Memories are essential to wizardry. By suppressing them, you suppress your ability to learn magic.' Lysander's words, spoken back in Solace.

A plump matron emerged from a cottage behind the priest. "Father Barnabas, there you are!"

"I just stepped outside for a bit of fresh air, Margaret," said the priest with a warm smile on his face. He glanced at Kyle. "I'm here to check on Margaret's daughter. Poor dear has a nasty fever." He let Margaret guide him into the cottage.

"Kyle, I'm waiting." Tia stood nearby. Vanessa exited the shop, one hand on Celina's collar.

Kyle bowed. "Of course, my lady." He helped the women into the wagon.

They resumed their journey towards Lupton.

There wasn't much to see – just fallow fields and the occasional solitary tree. There were more trees across the river, but the forest itself didn't start for a good couple of miles. He didn't see any good spots for an ambush or other unpleasantness – but given his wartime experiences, he didn't let that observation relax his vigilance.

War. Ambush. Pain. Death. Rotted corpses on a battlefield.

"Gah, what a stench," said Vanessa.

Kyle inhaled an aroma reminiscent of dead bodies and open sewers that went straight to his lungs and set them on fire. No. The fire came from his amulet. Bearak. He flicked his eyes across the landscape. Flat fields. Shed. River. Did bearak's swim? The water would kill the stench. Shed. And there, tied to a weathered stump-

"Kyle, that's a droath." Tia sounded exasperated. "Uglier, smellier, and more stupid than you. No, the droath is smarter than you. And it certainly doesn't drink."

Tia's tone made him wince. "Yes, my lady." He gave the droath a second glance. The six-legged, cottage-sized creature sported a red rug cast over leprous green-gray skin and a snout that diverged into a clutch of tentacles. Ugly as sin, but placid as a cow. A droath. Used to haul heavy loads across the Empire.

"It stinks worse than you," said the little girl.

Kyle realized the wagon was at a near halt. Ginger and Buttons stomped their hooves. The droath had them spooked. He flicked the reigns. The horse departed at a fast trot.

Some magician I am. Maybe I should stick with driving a cart.

EMPIRE: COUNTRY VII - Rebecca

Gypsies! I wonder which clan? Rebecca strolled from the castle in the early morning light, lyre case strapped across her back.

A clutch of colorful wagons across the river caught her attention. *Just four caravans? Pathetic.* The marks on the second wagon sparked a memory. *No, it can't be. I left them in Niteroi.* But Rebecca's feet carried her over the stone bridge despite those doubts.

She peered at the wagon that had caught her attention. *It is Hanja's wagon. But how?* The second wagon's shape and faded paint job sparked another memory. Cisco's wagon. Was he here? The third was a generic freight hauler, the sort that sold new in Xenon and used anywhere else. The last wain was a monster, its sides and top festooned with tiny cupolas and minarets. *It'd take a whole team to pull that abomination. Or a droath.* Rebecca's curled her lips in disgust. Droath could pull damn near anything. But they smelled worse than a sewer.

"Hola! Who are you?" The challenge originated from a thin, swarthy fellow wearing a purple vest over a white shirt and pants leaning against a tree.

Rebecca peered at the gypsy. His features and body shape sparked further dormant recollections. "Hiram?" Last she'd seen Hiram, he'd been sitting in a cell in Niteroi, along with the rest of her clan.

The man advanced in the jerky rhythm of a Dust addict. "How do you know – wait – Rebecca? Is that you?"

Rebecca twisted her features into a forced smile. Hiram had a reputation for duplicity and casual cruelty. "Yes, it's me, you great fool."

Hiram wrapped Rebecca in a hug. "How did you find us? Where have you been?"

Rebecca pushed the scrawny man away. "I have a new gig now. I'm maidservant to a merchant lord's daughter."

Hiram's face brightened. "Ah, the old honeypot scam?"

"Yes." Hiram lived in a world of scams and cons. The truth of Rebecca's relationship with Tia was beyond his comprehension.

A wagon door banged open. "How am I supposed to sleep with all this bloody racket?"

A large bare-chested man appeared in the doorway, rubbing his eyes. "Hiram? You found a woman? Here?" Disbelief rang in his voice.

Hiram faced the newcomer. "No, she found us. Rodrigo, it's Rebecca! She found us!"

Rodrigo peered at her. "By the powers, it is you." His lips widened into a broad smile. "That's good. We need another player."

"I have a gig." Rebecca trusted Rodrigo less than Hiram. Rodrigo thought he was the powers own gift to the opposite sex and grew violent when informed otherwise.

"She's running the honeypot on a merchant's daughter," said Hiram.

"Drop it." Rodrigo made a dismissive gesture. "We're blood."

"I'm expected back soon." Just like Rodrigo. No concern for anybody but himself.

Rodrigo waved his hand again. "Doesn't matter. You're people. They're not." His voice hardened.

Rebecca took the hint. Rodrigo saw others as kin or victim. Sometimes both. "How did you escape the slave pens?" The clan had been enslaved for brawling and petty theft. She'd escaped through her music and wit.

Both men stared at the dirt.

Discordant sounds reminiscent of bird songs, thunderstorms, and creaking trees emerged from across the encampment.

Rebecca discerned patterns within the bizarre melody. The tune sparked memories of the half-forgotten songs taught by Old Ruth,

Rebecca's musical mentor. The Church named such discordant combinations of notes 'Devil's Chords.' In ages past, witch hunters burned those who dared play such music. But even gypsies seldom played the Old Songs. Too wild. Too dangerous.

"He's awake already!" Rodrigo ended the statement with a flurry of curses and a hurled stone.

"Who?"

"The yellow bastard," said Hiram.

"The flute blower," said Rodrigo. "He came with the new boss."

Rebecca cocked her head. "New boss?"

Rodrigo kicked a stone and stared at the ground. "A Saban wizard. Thought for sure the slavers would take him just because-" the black folk were pretty much automatically slaves in Niteroi, "but instead, he sprung us. The ones still sucking air, anyhow. Got a couple of the caravans back as well." He looked at the dirt. "Then he made some changes." Was that a shudder?

Rebecca wondered who could cow an obstinate lout like Rodrigo.

A giant ebony skinned man appeared, garbed in tight leopard-skin breeches with a matching cape. Dreadlocks adorned with beads and coins framed his face. Yellow eyes filled with power and secrets pierced Rebecca. "Ah, a new arrival." The baritone voice might have originated from a bottomless well.

"Rebecca," Rodrigo spoke in a respectful tone. "A former member of the troupe. Before." He stopped short. Unspoken secrets hung in the air. "She's a player. A good one."

"Indeed." The black giant's lips curved into a smile. "True, Tamara is barely passable."

"Rebecca's way better than Tamara." Rodrigo's tone turned urgent.

The flutists piped a series of notes reminiscent of ghosts and lost souls. "That's the old music." The words escaped Rebecca's mouth of their own accord.

The giant's yellow eyes pierced Rebecca with such force she wavered on her feet. "You can play the old music." It wasn't a question.

"Yes." The eerie music dominated Rebecca's consciousness and made communication difficult. Flashes appeared in her mind: a barred spiral made of stars, a madcap city on a dark lake, and inhuman creatures gathered in a dark glade. Each just a hint.

"Old Ruth taught her a lot," said Rodrigo.

The ebony giant smiled and bowed from the waist. "I am Silam the Sorcerer, purveyor of ancient secrets, and expert in arcane mysteries. Permit me to introduce you to the flutist."

EMPIRE: COUNTRY VIII - Tia

Tia kept her face impassive as she regarded the skinny man before her. Gravitas. Dignity. That mattered before almost all else with the eastern aristocracy.

She stood in the Atrium of Castle Lupton; a square edifice built around a central courtyard. Three doors opened from this chamber: the main entry, a barred portal to Tia's left, and another across the room.

Steward Kessler stared down his skinny nose at Tia. "The Consul has no time for commoners."

Celina put herself in front of the steward and jabbed her finger. "You take those words back, sourpuss. Treaty says I can come here whenever I want and bring whoever I want. Well, I'm here, and I brought Miss Tia with me." With that, she marched right past the steward.

Vanessa looked stricken. "I-I need to watch her."

Kessler's vulpine head nodded a fraction.

Vanessa took off after Celina.

Tia kept her face impassive. "Mister Kessler, I request an audience with your master." She kept her tone calm.

The Steward stood his ground. "His lordship is occupied. You cannot expect him to rearrange his day on a whim."

Tia didn't budge.

The left door popped open. Sigrid, resplendent in a cream toga, entered the chamber. "Enough." He took in Tia's styled hair and rose-colored chiton, the side-less rectangular garment worn by women of means in the Eastern Heartland. "I am Consul Nigel Sigrid of Lupton District. You were with Ian yesterday." He put a finger to his chin. "Let me guess – a merchant's daughter from Equitant, scouring the countryside for profit and prospective husbands alike. Well, let's hear your pitch."

"My lord, I am Tia Samos, currently in service to Master Merchant Palo Rubinus." She kept her head aimed at the floor. The eastern aristocracy viewed uninvited eye contact from social inferiors as offensive. "This is not a proper venue for discussing our business."

"Well dressed and polite." The Barons head moved. "Dispatch a light repast to the triclinium."

Kessler departed through the far doorway. Tia's hidden apprehension diminished. She'd have preferred to meet in Sigrid's study, but the 'triclinium' or dining room would suffice for minor commerce.

"Follow me." Sigrid spun on his heel, nose raised, and marched through the doorway after his flunky.

Tia followed suit and found herself in a gallery dominated by portraits of former Consuls, all of whom seemed to sneer at the merchant's daughter.

"My esteemed ancestors," said Sigrid. "One should know one's antecedents."

Tia refrained from comment. Her paternal grandfather was a serf released from bondage by military service. Her maternal grandfather was a petty trader turned speculator. That combination made her much too common for the likes of Sigrid.

Sigrid opened the next door.

Tia surveyed the triclinium. Friezes of pastoral scenes dominated the walls, and an abstract mosaic covered the floor. A square table carved from cream-colored marble filled the room's center, flanked on three sides by lines of couches upholstered in purple and blue. Windows to Tia's right opened onto a central courtyard dominated by the square pool, or 'impluvium' common to eastern manors.

A blue-tinged flame from a metal cup in the fireplace caught Tia's eye. Fumar sap. Her brow wrinkled. Fumar trees were scarce. She should know. Fire trees formed the core of her family's prosperity. Entire forests of fumar trees were felled during the war, the hot burning logs used to feed wartime forges. Now, the precious trees were rationed, and the whole imperial economy suffered from that shortage. So, what was Sigrid's source? No fumar trees grew anywhere near here.

A servant placed a crystal carafe of wine and platters of bread and cheese on the table.

"After you, Lady Samos."

A test. An ignorant merchant's daughter would seat herself at the rear couch. Tia wasn't ignorant. Instead, she strode to the nearest right-side bench and laid down with her head cocked towards the table.

Sigrid walked around the table and reclined on the center couch.

A servant filled tiny cups with dark wine.

Sigrid lifted a glass. "I am informed Sir Peter Cortez is your escort."

"That is correct." Tia kept her voice neutral. "He was recommended as a capable guardian in Xenon."

The Baron sipped from his glass. "Yes, Sir Cortez is more than a match for the brigands and beasts that infest the highways." He sighed. "I understand he accompanies his brother to eradicate the bearak troubling this region."

"This is true." Tia reached for her cup.

"Slaying bearak's and other fell creatures is a Cortez tradition." Sigrid looked down his nose as he spoke.

Celina appeared in the courtyard with a youth who resembled a pale weed. She pranced along the pool's perimeter while the boy plodded behind her.

"My grandson Liam." Sigrid motioned to the couple. "Future ruler of the reunited Lupton District."

"Reunited?" Tia took a tiny sip.

"My dear, the separation between Lupton and Cosslet is entirely artificial." Sigrid selected a small loaf. "Ages ago, the Avar tribes invaded Cato province from the Kirkwood. The entreaties of Saint Andrew and spells of Jamison the Renegade halted the horde at Xenon's gates, but not before they established themselves in the Kirkwood."

Tia nodded. Old history. She plucked a biscuit from the platter.

"The Avar Warlords erected a chain of fortifications to secure their conquests. Cosslet Keep was one such, built by a chieftain of the same name. That chieftain's descendants, now styling themselves 'Barons,' ruled this region. Exposure to civilized folk softened the Avar savagery. Avar and imperial lines mingled. My grandfather married the Cosslet's last heiress. Then he built Castle Lupton. Cosslet Keep, old and worn even then, went to Dion Cortez, a collateral descendant of the old family.

"Dion proved ambitious. While my grandfather labored here, Dion visited the nearby Avar villages and persuaded them to swear allegiance to himself – a process much hasted by his killing of two bearak's and a troublesome werewolf. And thus, Cosslet became split in twain. My grandfather was rightly peeved – but as the new imperial line had Avar roots, his appeal fell on deaf ears."

"That is a most illuminating lesson," said Tia.

Sigrid's features remained fixed. "The Scrotti invasion decimated the entire province and the war taxes bankrupted those who failed to take appropriate action."

"Ah." Tia took a tiny sip. "My parents are fumar farmers who doubled the size of their plantation early in the war, ensuring a measure of prosperity afterward."

"Most commendable of them." Was that the tiniest of starts in Sigrid's voice?

"Thank you."

"Lord Cortez," Tia didn't miss the demotion, "while a genuinely decent soul, lacked the fortitude to take appropriate measures. As a result, he became deeply indebted. To forestall destitution, he approached me for financial surety. I agreed – on the condition the districts be reunited through marriage. On that day, Liam becomes

Consul of the reunited Lupton District while the Cortez clan retains ownership of only Cosslet town and castle."

"I see."

"Ian has received a string of wealthy young ladies of mercantile background since his wife passed away, each aspiring to become the new Baroness Cortez. Each departed once she learned of Ian's impoverishment and future demotion from 'Baron' to 'Lord.' I shall be clear." The Consul's voice assumed a hard tone with the last sentence. "Cosslet and Lupton Districts will be reunited."

"Consul Sigrid, my family advanced by seeking out opportunities and making a shrewd assessment of their risk. Unattached aristocrats such as Baron Cortez are worth investigation. But he is not the sole reason for my visit."

Sigrid remained silent for a prolonged moment. Then he nodded. "Outside investment may restore a measure of prosperity to my district. Therefore, I authorize you to seek business opportunities among Lupton's subjects. Kessler shall present you with a token at the door."

"You are most gracious, my lord." Tia rose to her feet.

Celina entered, trailed by Vanessa. "Liam is sick again." She faced the Baron. "You need to get him a real doctor, or I won't be able to marry him coz he'll be dead."

A vast sigh escaped Sigrid's throat. "I shall."

Vanessa guided Celina from the room.

"My lord, I'm sorry." Tia's voice radiated sympathy.

"Don't be." Sigrid sunk into the couch.

Kessler awaited Tia in the gallery, claw-like hand wrapped around a small packet. "Consul Sigrid's token and papers for your parents," he said.

Tia smiled. "Why thank you."

Kessler's perpetual scowl intensified. The hand holding the bundle didn't budge. "It's not a free service." He named a number.

Nor are loans. Those 'papers' were undoubtedly noble pleas for money. Tia had collected similar documents from each aristocrat on this tour. Rather than verbalize the thought, she reached into her purse and counted out the requisite coins.

A genuine smile appeared on Kessler's face as he transferred the packet.

The atrium door opened. Celina pranced into the chamber. "Hurry up! I want to see Master Anatoly."

"Of course," said Tia.

The drying sheds in Master Anatoly's yard were almost devoid of wood.

Inside, Tia observed a man sanding a beautiful armature while a second polished a row of dark chairs.

Tia addressed the polisher, a thin man in a leather apron. "I am Lady Tia Samos, here to see Master Anatoly. Is he available?"

The polisher bowed. "I shall fetch him."

Celina bounded into view. "He finished it! Come on. You gotta see!" With that, she latched onto Tia's hand and dragged her into an alcove.

"It's nice," Tia surveyed a miniature house perched on a table. The structure sported wooden walls painted to resemble stone blocks, arched windows, and battlements along the roof.

"See, it opens!" Celina touched a stud and pulled. The house split as though it were a book, exposing a detailed interior.

Tia spotted a formal dining hall, a kitchen with a stove and sink. She wondered who footed the bill. If this was what Ian spent his coin on...

Celina stuck her arm into an upper bedroom. "Wow, the beds have real blankets!"

A polite cough came from behind Tia. She turned to find a whip-thin man wearing a stained brown smock over a blue tunic.

The man bowed. "Lady Samos, I am Anatoly the Woodworker."

A tiny 'thud' marked the impact of a miniature bed with the floor. "It's not broken, is it?" Celina sounded concerned.

Master Anatoly's deft fingers plucked the toy and brought it close to his eyes. "No, it's undamaged." He carefully replaced the bed in the dollhouse.

Tia inclined her head at the toy structure. "Your craftsmanship matches its reputation."

A tight smile appeared on Anatoly's face. "I am flattered."

"I seek to invest in your enterprise on behalf of Master Merchant Palo Rubinus," said Tia.

The artisan patted his apron. "Perhaps we should discuss this in my office."

"Puppets!" Celina emerged from behind a crate. Strings connected her hands to a manikin in a white dress. A silver crown topped the figures golden hair. "See? A princess. There's others too – a knight that looks like Peter and a monster"-

"Celina! Put that back right now." Vanessa took a threatening step towards the girl.

Celina dodged. The puppets strings became entangled with the crate. "It's got me," yelped Celina.

Anatoly surveyed the scene. "An entertainer contracted me to repair those puppets for his performance tomorrow. A challenging task, as many were damaged by fire."

The artisan set the puppet knight on a crate. "This fellow's original weapon was an utter loss, I'm afraid. Melted." He reached into a nearby bin and produced a bronze blade with a flat hilt. "I shall outfit him with this one instead."

"Entertainer?" Vanessa unhooked Celina. "You mean Silam?"

Anatoly smiled. "Why yes. A most unusual fellow. My family looks forward to his performance."

"Wow!" Celina stepped away from the doll.

"I'll put this back." Vanessa glared at Celina. "Behave yourself."

The craftsman reached into an overhead cubby and produced two wooden dolls – a lady in a white dress, and a handsome knight in tin armor with a miniature steel sword belted to his waist. He presented the figurines to Celina with a flourish. "These, my dear, you can have straightaway. I shall deliver their dwelling on the morrow."

Celina's eyes widened. "Thank you!" She took the knight and dashed across the shop. Cries of, "Die, monster!" echoed from the aisles.

"Celina!" Vanessa's face colored.

"Oh, she'll be quite alright." Anatoly motioned at a doorway. "Lady Samos, my office awaits."

A cluttered but organized desk flanked by comfortable chairs dominated the artisan's office. Tia settled into a cozy chair with tan cushions while the woodworker claimed a spot behind the table.

"Master Anatoly," said Tia. "I find your craftsmanship impressive, but I could not help but notice the dearth of stock in your yard."

The artisan puffed his chest. "My woodcutters scour the Kirkwood for the finest trees. Once felled, the logs must be milled, and the planks seasoned for a year before use."

Tia gave him her best glare. "I am familiar with such requirements. Even so, your stock is scant."

Anatoly's eyes dropped. "There have been incidents with the cutters." The artisan spoke in a subdued tone.

"What sort of incidents?" Realization struck her. "The bearak."

Anatoly's face fell. "Yes, the bearak. Five men dead, and the Foresters rangers nowhere to be seen."

Tia leaned towards the desk. "And what did the Forester say?"

The door banged open behind her.

"The Forester," said Charles, "advised against logging in that location."

Anatoly raised his hand. "You said no such thing."

"Silence, peasant." Charles faced Tia. "You agreed to remain at Cosslet."

"No, I agreed to consider that advice." Tia kept her features fixed. She could not permit her authority to be usurped by a petty official.

Charles went red. Anatoly went white.

A slender arm draped itself over Charles' shoulder. "Come, dear, no harm done. Why get all excited?" Vanessa asked in a husky tone.

Charles pushed Vanessa's arm off his shoulder. "You should know better."

Vanessa pouted. "I don't know better. That's why you like me."

Tia spotted Celina behind the pair making a gagging motion.

Vanessa whispered in Charles' ear. The Foresters feature's relaxed as she guided him from the room.

Tia exhaled.

Anatoly cleared his throat.

Tia returned her attention to the artisan.

Master Anatoly hemmed and hawed but finally announced he could not accept Master Rubinus's gracious offer of partnership.

Tia thanked the artisan, rose to her feet, and departed the shop.

Outside, the wagon stood unattended. *Typical.*

Celina appeared. "Vanessa left with Charles. I bet they'll do icky things tonight."

Tia glared at the girl. "Into the cart."

Kyle emerged from a shuttered smithy, booze on his breath. Great.

EMPIRE: COUNTRY IX - Kyle

The nonstop gossiping and insults made Kyle's head pound. The hyperactive kid bouncing all over the wagon didn't improve matters. So, when the highborn entered the manor, he parked the wagon behind a shop and walked to the bar.

Naturally, the whole damn place gaped at him when he entered the taproom. Stupid uniform. Stupid Tia for making him wear it. He glared at the customers. They flinched away.

"Good day, fancy pants," said the barkeep, a grimy, balding slug in a sleeveless tunic and stained apron. "Here for a flagon of our finest vintage?"

"Beer." Kyle fumbled in his pocket and plopped a copper coin on the table.

"Not enough."

Highway robbery. Kyle dropped another copper next to the first.

The barkeep shook his head.

Screw this. Kyle emptied his pocket. Five coppers total. "Make it a double."

The barkeep started to open his mouth, thought better of it. He swept the coins into his apron and plopped a tall flagon brimming with foam on the table.

Kyle put the tankard to his lips and sipped. It tasted like piss. Thieving barkeep. Screw it. He drained half its contents in a single long gulp. A second gulp saw him looking at the cup's bottom.

The barkeep eyed him. "Thirsty today, ain't we?"

"More."

The barkeep's hands didn't move. "Got more coin?"

"I gave you enough coin for a whole damn keg of this rat piss, you worthless bastard."

A yard-long slab of oak sprouted from the barkeep's hand. "I don't take kindly to insults, fancy pants."

Kyle shifted in his seat. His meaty paw grasped the rods midsection. "Give me another, and I won't shove that stick up your ass."

The barkeep tried to budge the stick. Failed. His face colored. "Fine. One more tankard. Then you leave. I don't want my place busted up."

"Ok." Two flagons would get him buzzed.

The second tankard was only three quarters full and had dark specks floating in it. It tasted worse than the first. Kyle decided not to press the point. He drained it, strode from the bar, turned, and almost walked into a wagon parked in front of the smithy.

Kyle sniffed. An oily aroma arose from a canvas bundle in the wagon bed. It seemed familiar. Not just oily, but woody. He reached for the tarp.

"Hands off my cargo, asshole." A bushy-bearded lout with one hand wrapped in a bandage materialized in front of Kyle, glaring at him through bloodshot eyes.

"What is it, Willy," called a voice from inside the smithy.

"Got a big snooping galoot out here, boss."

Another bushy-bearded lout stepped into the street; hand wrapped around the hilt of a pig sticker. He looked familiar, somehow. "Leave now, mister. Don't let me catch you sniffing around my wagon again. Me an' the Consul is like this." He snapped the fingers on his free hand.

"Ok. I don't want trouble." He had plenty of that already. Kyle walked back to the cart, climbed onto the bench, sat, and thought. What was all that about? That smell. He knew that scent from somewhere. Kyle sat straight in the cart. Fumar wood. Fire trees were worth their weight in silver these days, or at least copper. No wonder the bushy-bearded louts were so uptight. Speaking of which, he remembered that voice. Bushy-beard had been at the warehouse yesterday.

So, Bruno's men were selling fumar logs. Where'd they get them from? There were supposed to be fire-tree groves left in Ambrose province north of here, but he couldn't envision their owners dealing with this crew. They might have found a cache, lost during the war. Unwelcome memories threatened to surface. Kyle rubbed his head. The half-formed images receded.

The fumar wagon rumbled towards the manor. He watched it trundle past the main gate. The driver was probably headed to a servant's entry.

A thought occurred to him. Bushy-beard wasn't willing to talk, but the smithy was another matter. He dropped from the cart.

The smithy was locked tight. He pounded on the door.

A dirty face materialized by the window. "We're closed. Go away."

Defeated, Kyle plodded back to the cart – and found Tia waiting for him, tapping her foot. The little girl poked at the wagon. He didn't see the other woman.

"You've been drinking." It wasn't a question.

"Yes, my lady."

"You're hopeless, Kyle." Tia threw her arms in the air. "Why do I keep you around?"

"I saw something." Maybe telling Tia about the fumar logs would get her off his back.

"What?" Tia's tone didn't soften in the least.

Hesitantly, Kyle reported his encounter with the bushy beards. Tia's expression turned thoughtful. She made him walk her to the smithy and pound on the door. This time, it opened a crack, just enough for her to exchange a few words. Then it shut.

Tia was silent on the walk back to the wagon. The kid, miracle of miracles, sat quietly on the driver's bench. The highborn slut was nowhere to be seen. Tia climbed aboard without assistance. "Take me back to Cosslet, Kyle."

Tia barely said a word on the return trip, even when Kyle hit three potholes in a row. Somehow, that was worse than the gossip and barbs.

EMPIRE: COUNTRY X - Peter

A branch snapped.

Peter winced. *Some monster hunting expedition this is.* The band created such a huge racket the damn bearak would hear its hunters coming a mile away.

The terrain didn't help their pursuit. Low but rugged hills capped with waist high brush and stunted trees surrounded the party, each capable of hiding a bearak – hell a whole tribe of bearak's. They fought their way through the bramble one step at a time. Branches whipped against the horse's legs and sides, making them skittish.

Yet, Charles insisted this was the bearak's route.

Charles. Peter's cousin rode a hundred yards ahead of the rest, a dark green blob in a gray tangle. Every few dozen paces, he'd stop, scan his immediate vicinity, and then point to another new grove or gully. Peter couldn't figure out what his cousin saw. Did Charles read the sign of the bearak's passage through this briar patch? Or did he merely guess?

As a boy, Charles had hunted hares, grouse, and doglike vree near Alexander's manor. Later, he'd graduated to stalking deer and wolves in the Kirkwood. Along the way, he'd become an excellent archer, a skill that served him well during the Occupation. Twenty-two goblins and barbarians fell to Charles arrows. Then, like Peter, he'd gone to the blood-soaked western battlefields. But while Peter became a knight, Charles followed a murkier path. Rumors placed Charles on missions of reconnaissance and assassination deep into enemy territory.

A rustle came from a nearby patch of brush. *Bearak!* Peter's hand shot to his sword hilt even as something small and brown shot through the bramble. Peter relaxed his grip. A rabbit, not a bearak.

That was another thing. An adult bearak was damn near as big as a cottage. How in hell could a creature that large move through this tangle without making a sound?

Rodriguez cursed. "I swear that bastard is leading us in circles." He nudged Jason Vasquez, then gestured at a large hill. "Don't that slope look familiar?"

Peter and Jason shrugged. Brush covered hills abounded, each almost identical to its companions.

Rodriguez and Vasquez didn't care for Charles guidance. They thought the bearak followed the overgrown Ochre Mine Road northeast instead of striking due north towards the Blight.

"Nothing for a monster to eat in the Blight," said Vasquez.

Carter opined indistinct marks in the trails muck looked like prints and ventured the monster headed east.

But Charles insisted the beast traveled north, and Ian had sided with him.

Rodriguez might have a point. Charles always did revel in others misfortune. 'What else to do but laugh when Fate gets back at people,' he'd say when challenged. That philosophy didn't apply to himself. When Fate turned on Charles, he became furious and berated those around him.

Ian's horse lifted a hoof and freed a flexible branch that snapped against Peter's armor with a 'ping.' Great.

Charles motioned from the summit of a nearby ridge. "I found something."

The hunters forced a path through the brush.

"Crap, that's the New Mire," said Rodriguez.

"Part of it." A smirk creased Charles' face. "Look at the far side." He pointed.

Rodriguez shaded his eyes and stared. "What?" The farmer's voice bore no friendliness.

"I see it," said Ian. "Those two dots near the marshes edge."

"Not dots, cousin," said Charles. "Dead cows."

Vasquez spouted a string of curses. "How did my cows cross this muck?"

"They must have panicked," said Rodriguez.

"Or the bearak carried them," said Carter.

"Well, nothing for it." Ian began to navigate a path towards the odious water.

Peter pointed at a muddy berm east of his position. "Is that the Ochre Mine Road?"

Rodriguez peered at the causeway. "Could be. I remember it crossed the swamp."

The decent was a pain. Hacking a path through the thick brush at the bottom was a bigger pain. Then they stood on a pair of ruts separated by knee-high weeds and interlaced vegetation above their heads.

Rodriguez glared at the swath. "This is the old Ochre Road. We shoulda just stayed on it and not let that damn idiot lead us on a bloody goose chase."

Charles' head swiveled at the comment. "Watch your tongue, peasant."

Rodriguez glared at Charles. "You shoulda kilt this damn beast a week ago. That's yer bloody job, ain't it?"

Charles turned and strode towards the farmer.

"Enough." Ian raised his hand.

Charles paused, then reversed course without a word. He strode over the muddy causeway without stopping. The others followed suit.

They rounded a corner and found large brown lumps strewn across the track. Not 'lumps,' Peter realized, but chunks of dead cows.

"Damn monster tore them apart," said Ian.

Charles continued past the carnage. "I spotted a trail." He vanished.

Rodríguez dismounted. He strode to the nearest mauled carcass. "What manner of beast does this? What creature possesses such strength?"

A demon. Peter's hand automatically moved to his breastbone, where Kyle's amulet pressed against his skin. Deliberately, Peter halted the movement. The charm remained cold. The demon was nowhere nearby. No! Bearak, not a demon, Peter reminded himself. The butcher was a bearak. It had to be a bearak.

Vasquez joined Rodriguez. He knelt by his slaughtered animal and flipped the carcass over with his boot. "No blood. The meat looks black."

"Bearak's suck blood through their tentacles," said Ian.

Demons also sucked blood.

"No flies, my lord," said Carter.

Peter blinked. The man at arms was correct. Bugs should have covered the carcass – even a carcass drained by a bearak. What was going on?

"Damn it! I can't even salvage the meat!" Vasquez kicked the corpse.

Hoofbeats announced the return of Charles. "Sure as stink, the trail goes right into the mire." Mud spattered his horse to the withers.

Peter responded with a phrase both impolite and anatomically impossible. He peered at the muddy water. How could Charles discern the beasts course?

Ian frowned as he stared into the swamp. "My ancestors hunted bearak's in the Kirkwood. Old stories say they lair in mountains or dark forests. But I do not recollect any tales of bearak's venturing into swamps."

"It headed into the swamp," insisted Charles. "What more do you want?"

Rodriguez stared at the dead livestock. "I got chores at home." His voice was subdued, mechanical.

"You can't be serious," berated Charles. "The trails fresh. We can kill it."

"The trail ain't fresh." Rodriguez raised his head and glared at Charles. "You done led us in circles all day. Enough is enough."

Charles went deadly still. "Are you calling me a liar?" He spoke in the deadly calm of a man about to lash out in rage. "Are you?" Charles jumped down from his horse and took three quick steps over to where the farmer stood and grabbed his shirt front.

"Take your hands off of me," said Rodriguez through clenched teeth.

"I said the bearak headed deeper into the swamp." Fury rose in Charles' voice. "I have spent my life tracking men, monsters, and beasts, and I know more about bearak's than you ever will." He shook Rodriguez for emphasis.

"Get your hands off me!" Rodriguez slammed Charles backward.

"You dare!" Charles reached for his sword. "You dare to lay hands on me! You worthless stinking"-

"Enough," said Ian.

Charles whirled on Ian. "You saw him. That peasant assaulted me."

"Settle down, Charlie." Ian only called his cousin 'Charlie' when he'd seriously screwed up. "We're all frustrated."

"You can't permit commoners to act like that," insisted Charles.

"Act like, what, exactly?" asked Ian. "He expressed a reasonable concern – the same concern I'd just stated. How is that insolence?"

"He's a peasant. You're not." Charles mounted his horse.

"Charles, he's frustrated." Ian's expression contorted in concern. "I don't hold that against him."

"Well, I do." Charles shot the farmer a malicious glare. "You can find the bearak without my assistance."

Ian watched Charles ride across the causeway. "Well, that could have gone better."

"Good riddance, begging your pardon, lord," said Rodriguez.

"Granted." Ian turned in place, unsure what course to take. "Any ideas?"

Vasquez cocked his head. "Think I hear something."

"What?" Ian turned his head.

Peter's right hand clasped his sword hilt. His left gripped the amulet. Still cold.

Vasquez smiled. "That's Elsa!"

Ian's face contorted in puzzlement.

"She's the smartest of my cows, my lord." Jason mounted his horse. "This way." He followed the track up the hillside.

They followed Vasquez along the overgrown track. Above them, something plowed through the brush.

"It's Elsa. I know it." Excitement permeated Vasquez's voice.

The trail reached a deep cleft and veered north. Peter spotted a brownish-red trickle of water in the gulches base. "Must be Ochre Creek."

"Down!" Carter slammed into Ian and knocked him from the horse.

"Ow!" Ian rolled onto his side. "Why'd you do that?"

The guardsman strode to a stunted tree, grabbed something, and yanked. "Somebody took a shot at us."

"Who?"-

"Leave. You're trespassing!" The shouted voice came from a distance.

Ian climbed to his feet. "I'm the Baron! Baron Cortez of Cosslet."

Distant, derisive laughter greeted his words. "Yeah, right! Get out of here, vagrants! These lands belong to Consul Brutus."

"Arrogant sots." Rodriguez glanced at Ian. "Begging your pardon, lordship."

Another arrow arched overhead and plowed into the brush a dozen yards from Peter.

Ian turned to Peter. "Damn fools. Let them have it."

"I see them." Vasquez notched an arrow.

"Me, too."

Peter spotted a brown dot on the far slope.

Arrows arced across the gap.

"Ah!" Brush thrashed across the gorge.

"Got him." Rodriguez lowered his bow with a satisfied smirk. "Ain't lost my touch."

"Damn you! You bastards hurt Willy."

"Leave, or we'll hurt the rest of you," Ian shouted.

"We'll tell Consul Sigrid about this."

"I told you; I am Baron Cortez." Ian shook his head. "Damned idiots." He looked at Peter. "What say we visit their warehouse tomorrow and explain to Consul Brutus's underlings that peppering their betters with arrows is a piss poor idea."

Peter curled his lips into a grin. "With pleasure, cousin."

Brush thrashed near the hill's summit, followed by a 'moo.' "Elsa," shouted Vasquez. "I'm coming." The farmer dashed up the slope, ignoring his horse.

Ian glanced at Peter. "Shall we?" He motioned at the hill.

Peter shrugged. "Maybe they reopened a mine."

"Not bloody likely." Rodriguez spat into the weeds. "My granddaddy worked that shaft, and it was almost spent even before the Scrotti killed everybody."

They remounted their steeds and followed the track until it dissipated in a weedy dell.

"Elsa!" Vasquez climbed towards a trio of cows cropping grass atop the ridge.

"I better go with him." Rodriguez set out after the other farmer.

A pair of irregular mounds caught Peters attention. Mine shanties reduced to wreckage.

Carter dismounted and walked to the nearest pile. He knelt and tugged a rusted scrap of bent metal from the heap. "Junk." He tossed the fragment aside.

Ian's head swiveled. "No sign of the bearak."

"Baron Cortez," Rodriguez called from the ridge. "We found something."

Ian shrugged. "Nothing here. Might as well look."

They dismounted. Knee high shrubs tugged at their breeches as they scaled the slope.

The farmers stood next to three cows atop the ridge. "I don't know what to make of it, my lord," he said as Ian crested the slope. "It's the Blight," said Rodriguez. "There shouldn't be anything."

Peter and Ian surveyed the terrain. The ridges opposite side dropped into a large basin.

"That should be the Blight," said Ian. "But where'd the forest come from? The Blight's supposed to be a lifeless waste."

"Nobody's entered the Blight in years," said Rodriguez.

"Strange looking trees," said Carter.

Peter silently agreed with the guardsman. The unnaturally straight trunks glittered in the sunlight, as though sprinkled with broken glass. Their cylindrical branches terminated in pointed clumps that resembled giant thorn plants. He put the tallest specimens at four times his height. "Sure is a bunch of them."

Ian scanned the ground near the forest. "I don't see any other plants."

"This is strange." A thought gnawed at Peter's brain. "This forest must be what Brutus's men guarded. But what tree could be so valuable?" Then he knew.

EMPIRE: COUNTRY XI - Tia

Neither the drab fields nor the carts jolting motion registered with Tia on the return trip to Cosslet. Instead, she was preoccupied with the conflicting thoughts that dueled in her mind: I can't be Baroness Cabbage. Cosslet is dreary and dull. Ian is naught but a titled beggar. Even my family's wealth might be insufficient to save him. But he is possessed of a better character than Lord Pervert or Lord Tombstone, and he's much easier on the eye than Sir Lard. He's also a full Baron – at least for now. That thought made her think of Sigrid. A schemer, through and through. Not at all like Ian.

A chill wind made Tia shiver within her cloak. The leaden clouds overhead promised chilly rain, possibly even snow. Snow. She hadn't seen snow since departing Equitant three years prior. Best to be indoors before a fire should that happen. Preferably a fumar fire. Fumar. That was another thing. Barnabas Brutus's band was dealing in fumar logs – but what was their source? The oaf thought they'd unearthed a forgotten cache, but she'd sniffed the air inside the smithy. Those logs were fresh cut. But the fire-tree groves hereabouts were felled during the war. The nearest extant grove was two hundred miles away in Ambrose province. So, where did these come from?

The cart struck a chuck hole and lurched. Tia's stomach lurched with it. She started to rebuke Kyle and then realized they'd reached Cosslet, and her stomach growled in hunger, not discomfort. She tapped Kyle's shoulder harder than was necessary to get the lumps attention. "I need to eat. Go to the inn."

Kyle grunted and steered the wagon into the village square. A large low building of cut stone filled one side of the triangular space, with a row of wains parked before it.

Celina pointed at the sign, featuring a four-horse coach in profile beneath the words 'Trevor's Roadhouse.' "I painted that. Pretty good, huh?"

Tia's gaze rotated between the child and the sign. "That's excellent work." Kyle helped her from the cart. "Shall we see what's on Master Trevor's menu?" Tia mentally prayed this roadhouse offered palatable fare.

Music wafted forth from the common room when Kyle opened the door.

Inside, sunbeams illuminated polished tables framed by padded maroon or green benches. A wagon wheel hung on one wall, while another sported a row of animal heads: boars, deer, and a bear. More tables and chairs stretched towards a stage at the rear where Tia spied the music's source: Rebecca, perched on a stool, strumming her lyre with closed eyes and a dreamy expression.

So, this is where the little tramp got off too.

A teenage girl in an apron and clean cream dress materialized and escorted Tia's party to a table near the stage, lit by a lantern set near an unobtrusive door. The server recommended their autumn special.

"What's that?"

The server smiled. "It's a hearty vegetable soup, my lady. The platter comes with bread, cheese, and sliced meats, all served fresh."

Hot soup sounded delicious. "That is acceptable."

The server bowed and departed.

Tia watched Rebecca perform while Celina fidgeted, and Kyle stared blankly into space – no doubt feeling the aftereffects of whatever rotgut he'd partaken of in Lupton. Well, it served him right.

Rebecca started a new tune. It featured discordant beats that made the hairs on Tia's skin rise.

"That's creepy." Celina stared at the gypsy. "It makes me see monsters."

Kyle rotated his head and gazed at the minstrel with a flat expression.

Tia had to admit the piece unnerved her. She half expected to see shadowy creatures walk from the wall.

Instead, the door alongside the table opened and a thin, sallow skinned man in a green robe emerged, carrying a flute. He tripped over a chair leg and fell onto Tia's table. His hand brushed hers.

An electric jolt ran through Tia. Lightning-fast images shot through her mind: a rugged mountain, a lighthouse atop a black cliff, a tiered city carved into a hill.

The man's eyes widened. He said something in a language that resembled birds chirping.

Chou, Tia realized. The flutist was from Chou, the strange nation across the world from Solaria. She'd studied the tongue at Solace, in anticipation of commercial contracts with the distant realm.

"Sorry, sorry." The words were in chou.

The flutist lifted his head. His eyes bored into Tia. More disjointed images assailed her: A village with square houses topped by oddly stacked roofs, a stone arch carved with fantastical images, and a huge mob of swarthy, black-haired horsemen.

"I – you – me." The flautist didn't look away from Tia.

Tia floundered. Lessons that seemed ages ago flashed into her mind. "Hello," she said in chou.

The Chou's face contorted. "You – me – remember?"

Realization struck. *The flutist wants to know if I remember him.* Strangely, Tia thought she should know this odd person. But she couldn't place him. A thought occurred to her – perhaps she'd encountered the fellow in Solace? The city did boast a miniscule Chou population. She remembered dining on shrimp and rice in a tiny chou eatery down by the docks. "You – Solace?" She used the imperial word for the city.

The flautist blinked and shook his head. "No. Elsewhere."

"Elsewhere?" Tia's mind raced. "Corber Port?" She'd seen Chou sailors on the docks of that mercantile city but hadn't interacted with them.

"No." He climbed onto the stage.

"The yellow man is strange," said Celina.

"He is," said their server, returning with a large platter. Steam curled from a trio of small bowls in their center. "They both are. That music gives me the willies." She sat the tray on the table. "They're with Silam's troupe."

Tia grimaced. "The gypsy is my maid."

The servers hand went to her mouth. "Oh, I'm sorry."

Tia smiled. "Don't be. Rebecca is prone to distractions."

On stage, Rebecca and the Chou entered a duet, the high-pitched flute clashing with the lyre's notes.

The server took in the scene with wide-open eyes. "That's not music at all. It's just noise." But she didn't leave the table.

"It is unusual." Tia absently plucked a carrot from the platter as she watched the performance. But she could almost detect a pattern in the bizarre mishmash.

"Enough," said a deep voice from beside Tia.

The music instantly seized.

Tia turned her head. She found herself gazing a giant, muscular man with coal-black skin wrapped in a sleeveless leopard-skin robe. She lifted her head and spied an aristocratic face dominated by yellow eyes and framed by colored dreadlocks twined with rings and strangely carved beads. The giant radiated presence and power. For an instant, he seemed more 'real' than his surroundings.

Tia gaped. *A Saban? How peculiar. Almost as peculiar as the Chou.* Saban's dwelt in the far southern jungles. Most in the empire were slaves in the harsh plantations of Niteroi.

"Master Silam!" Celina's squealed with delight.

The giant Saban tilted his head. His astonishing eyes seemed to bore into Tia.

"Ah, mistress...Celina, is it not? Baron Cortez's daughter?" His voice was deep, rich, and melodic.

"You remembered!" Celina clasped her hands together. "Can you show me magic? Please?"

"Perhaps." Silam's long dark fingers wove an intricate pattern above the table. Tia's heart raced as a column of luminous pink and cream mist sprouted from their tips and twisted together, becoming a miniature pale girl in a pastel dress. The phantasm made a pirouette and dissolved.

"That was great!" Celina grabbed Tia's arm. "This is Lady Samos. She's coming with me to your show tomorrow." Small fingers dug into Tia's flesh. "Right?"

The pain broke the spell of those yellow eyes. "Uh, yes."

Silam inclined his neck. "Pleased to make your acquaintance, Lady Samos." He spread his arms. "I am Silam the Sorcerer, Prince of the Untamed South, taking a tour of these distant northern realms." He smiled. "Well, distant to me, anyhow."

Tia finally composed herself. "I am Tia Samos, visiting here on business."

"Ah, a pleasure to encounter such a beautiful young woman." He took her hand and kissed it. "I anticipate your attendance tomorrow."

Heat rushed to Tia's cheeks. She opened her mouth, but no words emerged.

The giants gaze shifted to Kyle. "Ah, another practitioner of the erudite arts, I see."

Kyle lifted his head from the platter and stared at the Saban. Breadcrumbs tumbled from his mouth. His eyes widened. His head bobbed. He swallowed with difficulty. "Uh, yeah."

Celina spared a quick glance at Kyle. "You don't look like a wizard. You look like a big fat peasant."

"My dear, mages come in all shapes, sizes, and colors." Silam rested a hand on the back of Celina's chair.

"Celina, mind your manners." Tia found it easier to address the girl than the Saban sorcerer.

"Ok." Celina sat back in her chair and made a face.

Tia collected her wits and faced Silam. "I look forward to your performance."

"And I anticipate your patronage with immense pleasure." Silam lifted his head. "But now, however, mundane matters demand my attention." He snapped his fingers, and the two musicians descended from the stage and exited via the side door. The ebony magician followed them.

Tia took a breath and realized she was still holding the carrot.

"Gertrude, Gertrude, I don't pay you to stand around." The speaker was a short man in a fine gray and green sweater.

The server straightened. "Sorry, Master Trevor. I-I"-

"No excuses, young lady." Trevor pointed at a crowd of teamsters near the entryway. "Those gentlemen are hungry.

The server scurried towards the newcomers.

Trevor bowed at Tia. "I trust everything is satisfactory?"

Tia smiled. "I have no qualms with the service. The entertainment was intriguing."

Trevor made a face. "Ah, that. These traveling entertainers are a strange sort. Still, they'll be playing to a packed house. Will you be in attendance, Lady"-?

"Tia. Tia Samos of Equitant, seeking opportunities for investment."

"Investment?" Trevor pursed his lips. "Alas, I fear Cosslet offers few prospects. My finances are adequate. Tell me, have you visited Master Nickolas's establishment?"

"I have," said Tia.

"Hm." Trevor pursed his lips. "Perhaps you should approach John Cell."

Tia raised an eyebrow. "What trade does Master Cell pursue?"

Trevor smiled. "Several. John rents out wagons and river barges to merchants and farmers, along with an assortment of tools."

"Oh. An entrepreneur." Trevor's description sounded much like her maternal grandfather. "Where might I find Mister Cell's establishment?"

"John's shop is halfway along the road to Lupton, on the river side." Trevor smiled. "But he is currently dining at that table." He pointed across the room to a middle-aged man dipping a spoon into a bowl.

Tia smiled. "Thank you for the recommendation."

A shout from up front attracted Trevor's attention. "Pardon me, Lady Samos, but I must deal with this." He vanished before Tia could respond.

Well, that was informative, thought Tia as she turned her attention to the platter, only to find half of it vanished down Kyle's gullet. At least he didn't slurp her soup with the rest. She considered reproaching the oaf but decided it wasn't worth the effort.

A pair of weathered men ambled over to John Cell, who regarded them over his bowl. "John," called the taller and dirtier of the pair, "I see you conned a sucker into having you watch over his droath!"

Droath. Tia remembered the dilapidated shop with the droath from this morning. That must have been Cells establishment.

"Coin is coin," Cell grumbled. "If one is clever and works hard enough, one gets some."

"And how much coin are you gonna get," asked the second man. "It looks fit to find a mud pit right soon."

Cell put down his spoon. "That's for me to know."

"Fine, be that way." The pair ambled into the roadhouse's depths.

Master Cell seemed a prickly sort – but nothing ventured, nothing gained. Tia rose and approached the entrepreneur. "Master Cell," she began.

"Yes?" Brown eyes regarded her from within a craggy face. "What's a pretty bit like you want with an old codger like me?"

Tia didn't let herself be put off by Cell's uncouthness. "I seek investment opportunities on behalf of the master merchant Palo Rubinus. Goodman Trevor suggested you might be amiable to such a prospect.

"I might be." Cell dipped his spoon. "Trevor told you where my place is at?"

"He did."

"Good." Cell swallowed. "You can stop by tomorrow." He pushed the bowl away and rose to his feet.

Tia watched him leave, and then returned to her table, where Kyle eyed the last few carrots and sole remaining biscuit.

"He sure eats a lot, doesn't he," said Celina.

Tia nodded and plucked a carrot from the tray. Cell wasn't much of a prospect, but he was willing to talk. Better than nothing. 'Nothing' summed up her experiences in Cosslet. She couldn't marry Ian. The local merchants didn't care for her. And the marauding monster didn't help matters, either. She ate a couple more carrots, drank a glass of weak wine, and finished off the biscuit. Tia rose to her feet. She decided to peruse Cosslet's market.

Bright sunlight made Tia wince as she stepped into the market as dense clouds tracked away to the north. The meager selections in the few booths didn't help her disposition: tin cooking ware, ribbons, workman's clothes, tools – about what she expected to find in a hick town. Depressing. Give her the markets of Solace or Corber Port any day.

God above, she could really stand a hit of Dust.

A ruckus from a tent on the markets western perimeter caught Tia's attention: a dumpy woman in livery arguing with the stall's keeper, a short, ugly middle-aged woman whose unkempt hair resembled a rat's nest. The customer looked familiar – yes, she'd been among the servitors at Sigrid's manor. Why would his servant's shop in Cosslet instead of Lupton?

Tia approached the tent just as the servant departed, face twisted into a scowl. Tiny jars littered the table. Bundles of leaves and roots dangled from the tent ceiling. An herbalist.

A small hand tugged at Tia's sleeve. "That's Mother Shrub. You don't want to see her." Celina sounded nervous.

"And why is that?"

"She's an ugly witch that lives in the forest." Celina refused to relinquish her grip. "She sells bad things."

Tia eyed the herbalist. Mother Shrub was certainly ugly – a short, twisted body topped by a head dominated by a pockmarked face almost lost in a wild tangle of salt and pepper hair. But if she had Dust – Tia broke Celina's grip and started for the stall.

"Don't go." Celina sounded on the brink of tears.

Stupid brat. But trepidation filled Tia's body as she neared the stall.

"What you want, dearie?" The proprietress leered at Tia.

"I – uh – do you stock Blue Dust?" It didn't seem likely.

The woman's eyes narrowed. "Travel weary, are we dearie? Looking to while away the miles?"

Tia nodded.

The herbalist shook her head. "Don't got any. Blue Dust is a southern drug." She smiled, exposing rotted and broken teeth. "But I got something better – Bliss Root."

Tia frowned, remembering her prior experiences with Bliss Root. Nausea. Headaches. Strange dreams. "Anything else?"

"Ah, a discriminating sort." The herbalist's smile remained fixed in place. "Mother Shrub likes that, I do."

Just like I thought. Tia started to turn from the table.

"Wait," said the herbalist. "I don't got Dust, and yer too prissy for Bliss, but I do have something else – Sweet Milk."

"Never heard of it," said Tia.

"It's from the west. The pasties use it."

Pasties. A slang term for the pale skinned Kitrin. "Kitrin is a thousand miles from here. How did you obtain it?"

"Oh, Mother Shrub has her sources, I do." The woman's smile stretched from ear to ear. Her head bobbed like a child's toy.

A shiver ran through Tia's body. *She's demented. But – my Dust is almost gone. One dose won't hurt.* "How much?"

Mother Shrub named a price. Tia cut it in half. The herbalist cackled and dropped her offer. Tia scowled and offered a fraction less. Mother Shrub presented her with a tiny vial no larger than a finger joint full of cream-colored fluid laced with green and black specks.

"One drop, no more," said the herbalist as Tia pocketed her purchase.

Transaction completed; Tia stared across the market at Cosslet Keep. No point in staying here.

Celina was sitting quietly in the cart when Tia climbed aboard. "You should throw that away." She spoke in an intense tone.

"You don't even know what I bought."

"It doesn't matter. It came from Mother Shrub, and she is evil." Celina crossed her arms and stared straight ahead.

Kyle flicked the reigns.

Ian waited just inside the castle gate, clothes dirty and scratched. But a smile played across his lips. "How did your day go, my lady?"

What's he so pleased about? Did they kill the bearak? "My Lord Baron, today was a most wonderful exercise in frustration."

The baron helped her from the wagon. "We must speak. I have news."

"What sort of news," asked Tia, but the Baron already strode towards the keep.

"This." The nobleman presented her with a tree branch.

What? Recognition struck. Not a tree branch. A fumar branch. Tia's heart pounded. "You have my attention."

Ian smiled. "We'll talk in my study."

Heart pounding with anticipation, Tia followed the nobleman into his castle.

"The trees must cover the whole blight and range from mere bushes to specimens more than twenty feet tall," said Ian, gesturing at the map behind him. "Forty square miles, split between Cosslet and Caestoninus."

Tia studied the map. "That is large." Larger than her family's farm. "How did the forest remain unknown for so long?"

"We think Uncle Alexander – the old Lord of Groveton - conspired with Julius Caestoninus to plant the trees prior to the Occupation." Ian glanced at Peter, who nodded in agreement. "Anyhow, we were away being schooled in Cato that year, and Groveton was massacred a fortnight after our return, along with the entire populace of the Caestoninus estate. Nothing would grow in the Blight, and the Caestoninus lands barely supported anything. Before the invaders came, their income came from dyes distilled from the old tailings."

"That would be what attracted Brutus's attention," said Tia. "His wealth comes from textiles. He made uniforms during the war."

"That makes sense," agreed Ian. "His agents must have ventured into the Blight looking for tailings and found the forest. But what were the trees doing there in the first place?"

"Fumar trees require tainted soil in which to thrive," said Tia. "In the north, we bring in wains filled with mine waste to saturate the ground – it acts as fertilizer."

Ian gave Tia a blank look. "I didn't know that."

Tia turned her lips in a slight smile. "Fumar farmers do not advertise that tidbit. Your relatives, though, appear to have deduced that fact – it speaks to their cleverness."

"Alexander was a smart one," said Peter.

Ian's face contorted. "But why keep the forest secret? To drive up prices?"

"Probably. He would also have needed permits and labor." Tia returned her attention to the map, calculating distances. "I must inspect the trees for myself. Can we reach the grove and return before dark?"

A tight smile appeared on Ian's face. "Barely. But we must depart straightaway. The road ends in thick brush three miles shy of the forest."

"I shall change into more appropriate attire." Tia looked at Peter. "Have Kyle ready the wagon."

Tia dashed to her room and threw open her trunk. From beneath her other garments, she extracted an outfit she'd not worn since leaving Equitant: a pair of sturdy tan breeches, irredeemably stained in the knees, and a thick woolen sweater. A pair of heavy boots completed the ensemble. Tia changed into the outfit and regarded herself in the mirror. Images of traipsing through the fumar trees with friends she'd not seen in years flashed through her mind. She secured her hair with a clip and exited the room.

Kyle was in the courtyard, leaning against the wagon, talking with Amelia. Celina pranced around them both like a demented rabbit.

"I like you," Amelia told the lout.

Celina stuck her head between the pair. "Are you going to marry him?"

"Enough." Ian emerged from an outbuilding, carrying a crossbow. Tia remembered a dangerous beast remained on the loose as Ian motioned at the cart. "After you, my lady."

Baron Ian helped Tia into the wagon and then climbed in after her. The cart jolted into motion almost immediately.

The road went from gravel to dirt within the first mile, and further degraded into parallel ruts another mile past that. Kyle, naturally, found every pothole. "This road will need rebuilding," Tia told the Baron after a quick grab on his part kept her from being hurled clear out of the cart.

"It'll be worth it." Ian maintained his grip as the wagon lurched again.

They passed a final ramshackle farm where three withered men raked dead plants into a pile. "Tull's Place," said Ian. "The end of civilization."

Tia judged they were just three miles from the castle. "How much further?"

"Two miles to Grove Creek," said Ian. "Then we turn east. The forest starts about three miles past that."

"And we must walk those last three miles." *The Fumar forest is eight miles from Cosslet Keep. What did it say about Ian that he remained ignorant about the lands so close to his home? What else is he ignorant of hereabouts?*

The track topped a hill. Ahead, the ground descended towards a brown stream. Shrubs and stunted trees lined its banks.

Ian pointed at a blackened stone structure. "The River House. Used to be an inn."

Tia eyed the ruin, which lacked its roof and part of one wall. "It could stand some repairs."

"It could." Ian tapped Kyle's shoulder. "Watch for a blue pennant on a pole. Turn there."

Kyle grunted and flicked the reigns. He steered the cart from the track onto a literal path, nothing more than a strip of packed dirt. Grass and branches slapped against the wain's sides. The trail climbed a series of slight slopes, while the creeks banks grew narrower and steeper. Finally, they reached a dell dominated by a shallow lake.

Ian pointed at a rubble heap near the pond. "Lord Alexander's manor. What's left of it, anyhow." He shifted his arm towards a grove. "Apple trees. I found them last year. I've not been past this point until today."

Well, Ian at least attempted to survey his lands. That counted for something.

Kyle guided the wagon past the ruin to a tiny clearing where the track vanished into the brush. "I'm afraid we must walk from here," said Ian. "Getting the horses through this tangle was difficult. I don't care to subject them to the experience twice in one day."

Tia eyed the twisted plants. Those branches would tear her clothes to shreds. But she had to see the fumar trees for herself. She leaped from the wagon without being helped. "Lead on, my lord."

"This way, my lady." Ian pointed at a distant line of hills. "It's easier to walk along the streambed."

Peter pushed aside a leaning sapling twice Tia's height, exposing a muddy ditch with a trickle of water in the bottom. Ian stepped through the gap and promptly sank in muck past his ankles.

Tia decided she'd have to burn the entire outfit after this expedition.

Branches slapped at Tia's arms and face. Mud stained her pants to the knees. Her legs ached. Sweat glued the shirt to her back. But she didn't dare complain. Then, finally, when her world was reduced stings and pain and mud, the column stopped moving.

Tia bent over, gasping for breath. Her body ached all over.

Voices reached her from above.

Tia lifted her eyes. The gully ended in a 'V' shaped notch at least thrice her height.

"We're almost there." Ian pointed at the slope. "Can you manage this?"

"I'll try," said Tia between breaths.

A frown crossed Peter's face. "Kyle."

The big oaf faced him, dirty but not winded by the exertion.

"Carry Tia."

Tia was too tired to object. Kyle knelt. She put her hands on his shoulders. Then he stood as though she weighed nothing.

Peter scaled the slope, and Kyle followed, apparently not perturbed in the least. A moment later they crested the lip and stood beside a small pond. Gray hills dotted with weeds stretched around them.

Tia slid to the ground. "Thank you, Kyle."

The big man grunted but said nothing.

Ian spun slowly around, taking in the view. "Follow me."

Clumps of prickly plants tugged at Tia's ankles. She kept having to raise her legs high to scale berms and boulders. Each slope they summited revealed only another hill past it, or worse, a gully followed by a hill. But the wind was worse. It cut through her clothes like a knife. Tia kept her head down to minimize the chill.

Ian stopped, and Tia almost walked into him.

"There."

Tia raised her head and squinted at clumps of spiky shapes rising from an orange plain otherwise devoid of life. They were two hundred yards off. Stunted. Twisted. Immature. But, despite the distance, Tia knew the shapes for what they were. After all, she'd been raised among their kin. Fumar Trees. The exhaustion fell from her limbs. The pain receded.

They strode into the wood. The outlying trees barely reached Tia's knees. After three hundred paces, they passed clumps of specimens taller than Kyle. "These are about ten years old." Tia tapped a shimmering trunk and received a metallic echo in response. "They're not ready to harvest." Strictly speaking, that wasn't true. The pulp within the younger fumar burned, but without the intensity of the mature trees.

Tia paused, hands on hips. "We need a count. Sir Peter, would you kindly plant that spear here?" She pointed at a spot by her feet, and the knight drove the shaft into the earth.

Tia turned her attention to Kyle. "Can you count?" When the big man nodded, Tia pointed east. "Walk that way. Count each stride. Stop when you reach a thousand." She faced Ian. "I shall count the trees to the right. Would you tally those to the left?"

Ian appeared momentarily baffled. "How deep?"

"Just those closest to our line of march?"

"I can do that."

Tia faced Kyle. "Begin."

"Yes, my lady." Kyle took a step. "One." Another step. "Two." At 'five' Tia started after him, counting the trees to her left as she walked, categorizing them by their heights. Ten or twelve times she had to sidestep the trunks in her line of travel. Thrice, she tripped over roots or rocks.

"Nine hundred ninety-eight. Nine hundred ninety-nine." Kyle took a final pace and halted. "One thousand."

"These trees are bigger than the others," said Ian.

"They're mature."

"Ready to harvest?" Eagerness filled the Baron's voice.

"Yes." She cast a glance at Ian. "What's your tally?"

A sheepish smile appeared on the Baron's face. "I-uh-lost count."

Ian needs to work on his mathematics.

"Three hundred twelve large ones," said Kyle. "Six hundred twenty about my size. I couldn't keep track of the saplings."

Tia and Ian gaped at him. Kyle's tally was close to hers.

"He's smarter than he looks," said the Baron.

"Indeed." Tia tapped her foot. "Anything else?"

Kyle motioned back at the ridge. "It'll take a full cohort of men two months to punch a canal through those hills. Plus, another month to dredge that creek and make a tow path."

"And you know this how?" Tia glared up at Oafs round face.

Kyle's confidence evaporated. "The army," he mumbled. "We dug a canal, once."

Tia remembered something Kyle said when she'd hired him. "You served in the II Equitant, correct?" That unit was renowned for their engineering skills.

"Yes, my lady."

"My uncle served in that unit. Olson Samos. Did you know him?"

"Yes." Kyle kicked at the dirt.

"A cohort." Ian wobbled on his feet. "That's five hundred men. Cosslet and Lupton together don't have two hundred laborers, not to spare, anyhow. Even bringing in workers from Overton and Oak Hill wouldn't be enough."

Oak Hill. Yes, Baron Osmic. Hadn't he been concerned about a fire that decimated that town? Tia put a hand on the Baron's shoulder. "That, my lord, is why you need me. My family possesses expertise in these matters."

"I – I guess I do." Ian seemed flummoxed.

"We'll discuss the details back at the keep."

They reached Cosslet just as twilight turned into darkness. Tia and Ian talked over fish, cabbage, and ale at dinner, and drew preliminary papers afterward in Ian's study.

Even then, Tia's energy didn't diminish. She fell into bed with her thoughts a swirl. I'm getting married to a bumpkin Baron. Married? Me? Baroness Cabbage? She shook her head. No. Baroness Fumar. I will transform Cosslet from a backwater village into a true town. The thought mesmerized her. She stared at the ceiling, wide awake. I must sleep. Tomorrow will be busy.

Her eyes fell on the tiny vial she'd purchased earlier. Perhaps that will help. Just one drop. She stuck a pinky finger into the container. The liquid touched her lips. Sensations flooded her mouth: Creamy. Bitter. Sweet. So very sweet. She swallowed.

Images flashed through her mind as consciousness receded.

EMPIRE: COUNTRY XII – Li-Pang

Li-Pang stuck his head into the cottage. "Mom, I'm off to pick melon berries."

"I will make them into jam." Mara, his mother, lifted her head from a green bowl. The left sleeve of her pale orange tunic fell back, exposing a spiral tattoo.

Li-Pang stared at her. Mara's last three attempts to make melon berry jam had been disasters.

Mara sighed. "Never fear. Yampi will help me this time."

Li-Pang exhaled in relief and started for the door. Yampi made good jam.

Outside, Shoo-Pang fitted a board into the goat shed. "Do not dally," he told his son as Li-Pang ducked behind Kura-Tan's shanty. From there, he took an almost invisible path through thick brush to Little Reed Creek, where he hopped from stone to stone across the stream – an accomplishment few other boys in the village could duplicate. He hoped this route would keep the bully Nan-Tang and his henchmen from spotting him.

Li-Pang reached a forked tree and grabbed a thick branch just above his head and touched a bamboo cylinder. As he brought his hand back down, the paleness of it registered in his mind. "Why am I so different?"

The answer was obvious: physically, Li-Pang took after his thin, pale foreign-born mother rather than squat, broad-faced Shoo-Pang. More than physical differences set him apart from Reed Villages other inhabitants.

He contemplated the cylinder – a laboriously carved flute that had taken him six pieces of bamboo to get right and slipped it through his leather belt. He'd managed to teach himself three songs since the traveling musician had come through last month – well, two and a half, really, since he'd never gotten even half the notes right for that shepherd song.

He strode along the faint path just past the tree to the melon berry patch.

Li-Pang set the bark bucket on a flat white stone. It was half full of berries – well, maybe not quite half full, but close. But this section was picked clean. He knew that the way he often knew the weather would shift or if dangerous animals were nearby. No choice. He had to visit the other patch. That meant passing by one of Nan-Tang's hideouts.

Li-Pang shuddered and hoped the bully was preoccupied elsewhere.

Alas, Nan-Tang was nearby, parked on a fallen log with two of his cronies. They had bark buckets at their feet, but red torpa root stained their lips.

Li-Pang shrank into the undergrowth, hoping the bully hadn't spotted him.

Nan-Tang dashed that hope. "What you doing here, Dead Boy?" 'Dead Boy.' The crude moniker he'd assigned to Li-Pang because of his corpse-like appearance.

"Picking berries." Li-Pang fought to keep his voice calm. Perhaps Nan-Tung would be content with insults.

"You mean stealing our berries." Nan-Tang hefted a heavy branch. "You must be punished."

Nan-Tang intended to beat him to a pulp. Li-Pang spun. His foot came down wrong. The road rushed to meet his face.

"Hah – Dead Boy can't even walk right." The bully's companions chuckled at his jest.

Li-Pang flipped into a sitting position. His side burned with pain. He imagined that pain multiplied by the wood of Nan-Tang's club. He saw himself crippled, cast out, dying alone, and nobody mourning his passage.

Li-Pang pulled the flute from his robe, now cracked, and stained with blood. Impossibly, the sight calmed him.

"You gonna try sticking me with that?" Contempt filled Nan-Tang's voice.

"No." Li-Pang felt his mind expand. "I'm going to play you a song." And he brought the flute to his lips.

Five twisted notes emerged from the broken flute.

"That's just noise." Nan-Tang's features contorted.

Li-Pang blew into the instrument. But it's cracked side distorted the sound. He shifted his grip to compensate – and found an alien sequence.

Nan-Tang halted and laughed. "Dead Boy thinks he's a jester."

Li-Pang drew a deep breath. He focused on the strange pattern. Blew. His fingers played over the tube's holes. The flute spat forth unearthly music.

"What is that?" Nan-Tang's club dropped to the road. He covered his ears. "Play something else, Dead Boy." His voice wasn't contemptuous anymore. Instead, it was tinged with fear.

Li-Pang ignored him; swept away by the song he was discovering note by note. Likewise, he didn't register the sudden wind and darkness that encompassed the road. Nor did he hear' the screams of Nan-Tang and his companions.

Finally, Li-Pang's breath ran out. Light and sound seemed different. And Nan-Tang was gone. He did, however, see his bucket of melon berries by the roadside.

Li-Pang rose and walked towards the bucket. Darkness on the ground caught his eye. "Why do I have two shadows?"

EMPIRE: COUNTRY XIII – Kyle

It had been a while, thought Kyle as Amelia's warm weight shifted beside him. He couldn't fathom what the woman saw in him. She wasn't put off by his size or scarred face – though she had gently chided him about drinking.

Amelia stirred again. Time to rise and face the world. Kyle rotated in place and sat, feet touching the chill floor. A bit of focused energy ignited the remnants of last night's fire.

"I like watching you do that." Amelia rose to a sitting position, exposing her large, flat breasts. "It's useful."

"Thank you." Kyle shrugged into his trousers.

"Sleep well?" asked Amelia. "No dreams about the war?"

"Yes." That had been a blessing, being able to shut his eyes without reliving moments of blood, black magic, and death. Perhaps Amelia was responsible. Her special brand of sorcery.

Kyle finished dressing. Time to face the day. He took a step towards the door.

"Wait." Amelia rummaged through a small box. "Here." She held out a plain copper ring. "It belonged to my man."

The world shifted beneath Kyle's feet. "Are you sure?"

Amelia smiled. "I'm sure. You need a place to settle, and I'm tired of being alone."

"I'm ugly."

"Not on the inside." Amelia reached for her dress.

"I am contracted to take Tia to Corber Port."

Amelia gave him another peck on the cheek. "Come back when you're done."

"But my nightmares"-

"Bad dreams plague Cosslet's other veterans. They talk to Father Barnabas. It helps."

Kyle pursed his lips. The notion still sounded ridiculous. "I'll think about it."

"Do that." Amelia pressed the ring into his palm.

Kyle stuck it in his pocket. Together, they exited the servant's dormitory.

In the courtyard a man unloaded a bicycle from a flatbed wagon.

Amelia greeted the fellow with a nod. "Thomas! What brings you here?"

"This." Thomas plopped the bike on the ground. "The baron asked for it."

The bike was what they called a 'glide' in the army because of the way it glided along rough roads. Much better than the biter's he'd peddled during his stint, so called because the chain would sometimes bite one's legs.

Kyle nodded in approval. "Looks good."

Thomas nodded. "Yep. A gift from the army." He turned his head and spat. Most veterans of the Traag War received imperial citizenship and near worthless tracts of land in Drakkar or Kitrin instead of coin. Thomas, it seemed, fared differently. He'd probably landed one of the vacant farms hereabouts. God knew, there were enough of them.

Amelia motioned at the keep door. "Join us inside for breakfast? I know you like Marta's cooking."

Thomas cast a glance at the door. "I'd like to, but Pa's waiting on me." He heaved himself onto the wagon and flicked the reigns.

Amelia and Kyle entered the keep. To his surprise, lazybones Tia was already at the table, hunched over a notepad, a steaming mug of something next to her elbow.

Tia raised her head. "You're here. Good. Has the bicycle been delivered?"

Kyle blinked. "Yes, my lady."

"You know how to operate it?"

"Yes, my lady." Of course, he knew how to drive a bicycle. He'd only pedaled the contraptions across half the empire.

"Good." Tia tore a sheet from her pad and thrust it at him. "I need you to take this to the signal tower at Stone Hollow. Can you accomplish this task by midafternoon?"

Seventeen miles to Stone Hollow. Another seventeen back. Thirty-four miles total. A dawn to dusk march for a man afoot. Half a day's ride on a bike. And that was with a Biter, not a Glide. "Yes."

Tia paused. "My carriage should be repaired. If so, bring it here."

"That will require money, my lady. I'll have to rent a horse. And it might take me until afternoon to return here." A thought occurred to Kyle. "Perhaps I should return the cart?"

"I have plans for the cart."

"Huh?"

"I intend to harvest three or four fumar trees after the Equinox." Equinox. A polite way of saying 'Hell Day.' Nobody sane would be doing anything tomorrow except hiding in church.

"Oh." Dammit. One guess as to who'd be pigging the logs through those hills.

Tia extracted a coin pouch from her dress – a simple rose-colored garment without frills – and stared into space for a moment. Then she counted out a stack of dinar. "Here. This should suffice."

Marta dropped a pot of porridge on the table. A younger girl trailed her with a platter of fried eggs and slabs of ham.

Kyle dug in. He'd need the energy.

Breakfast completed, Kyle returned to the dormitory, slung the crossbow across his back, and belted on the shortsword. Back in the courtyard, he grabbed the bikes handlebars and started to throw a leg over the frame.

"Forgetting something?" Tia stood in the keep entry, with an irked expression on her face.

"Huh?"

"Kyle, your uniform. You represent me on this trip and need to dress appropriately."

Kyle sighed. "Yes, my lady." He dismounted and lumbered into the dormitory where he shrugged into the all too familiar jacket, boots, and cap.

Feeling ridiculous, he strode back into the courtyard only to be ambushed by Amelia, who wrapped her arms around his neck and pecked him on the chin. "Come back safe. Don't let the monster get you." She pressed a wineskin at him.

"I won't." He clenched the skin and hugged her back.

Tia cleared her throat.

Kyle released his grip, mounted the glide, and started pedaling, gaining speed almost immediately. Damn, this machine was a wonder, way better than a biter. He flashed past Cosslet, dodged a hay wagon, and then he was in farm country. A once familiar burn settled into his legs halfway between the villages. God above, he missed this – riding a bike had been among his few pleasures during the war. He had to be doing ten miles an hour!

The highborn dismissed bicycles as conveyances for commoners. In their eyes, true aristocrats traveled by horse-drawn carriage. More fools they, in Kyle's view. Bicycles reduced a day's walking to a couple of hours pedaling. Even cavalry had difficulty keeping that pace. And bikes didn't need god-awful amounts of hay, either.

Kyle shot past apathetic peasants and pathetic huts alongside the road as he flashed through Lupton. Men and women beaten low by arduous work and cruel scorn; such was life under Lords like Sigrid. The sight, as before reminded Kyle of his youth in Bestia, a time of beatings and starvation and hard labor. But, ultimately, Lord Atticus, despite his claims of superiority, proved far more brittle and fragile than his subjects.

Then Lupton was behind him, and he crossed fallow fields towards the looming bulk of the Boundary Tree. No sign remained of the massacre. But Kyle eyed the brush to either side as he dropped into the swale and shot over the Ochre Bridge. The rise killed his velocity, but no matter, Kyle's feet pressed the pedals and the wheels turned, and he soon attained the summit.

Nothing moved at Brutus's warehouse. The building itself was shut tight and lightless, a blank cipher in a bleak landscape. Kyle didn't slow his pace but plowed on full tilt, now climbing, now descending, eyes flicking from the road to brush covered slopes.

Ahead, the brush rustled.

Bearak? The hairs along Kyle's neck rose. That wretched beast, whatever it was, was still out there. The brush there was tall and thick, enough to conceal the beast. He drew nearer, spotted a dull horn attached to a bovine head; a cow munching on leaves.

Kyle pressed on. A dozen miles done, five to go, but his throat was raw, he needed to piss, and the hot pain in his legs had become an inferno. He stopped atop a hill and extracted the wine skin. Liquid coursed down his throat. Kyle gagged and almost spat the fluid from his mouth - Amelia had filled it with water, not wine. To Hell with it. It still quenched his thirst. He drained the sack, stretched his muscles, and watered the weeds. Then he climbed back on the bicycle.

Farms appeared among the rolling hills. One rise stood out among the others, a gray lump with a splintered spike protruding from its summit: the curved peak that gave Stone Hollow its name, and its attendant signal tower.

Armed men stepped from the trees as he approached the town.

"Nice bike," said one, a fellow with a gap in his teeth. "That's a glide, right?"

"That's some serious weaponry yer lugging," remarked a flat faced man with a bill cap. "Mind telling us why?"

Kyle scowled at the pair. "Bearak. Near Cosslet."

Missing Teeth whistled. "We heard about that. Been a dog's age since the last one came out of the woods. His lordship sent men into the hills looking for it."

"Thoughtful of him," said Kyle.

"Dead peasants don't pay taxes." Bill Cap turned and spat. "You running messages for the gentry?"

"I am." Kyle patted the bag. "Got one for the signal tower."

Bill Cap motioned at a side road cut into the ridge. "That'll save yew some time."

The summit granted Kyle a view of a burg laid out in concentric circles within a stony crescent. Above him, the tower's semaphore arms, three to either side, jerked like the legs of an uncoordinated spider.

He removed Tia's missive from his pocket and stared at it. EAC4. FF30SM. QS96100. L360000M. PCTB. WFN, plus a destination code. Thirty-six letters and digits. To the untrained eye, it was a mishmash of numbers and letters without meaning. But he could puzzle it out. EAC4 – 'Engagement Agreement Candidate 4.' FF30SQ – 'Fumar Forest 40 Square Miles.' QS 96,100. L 200,000M – 'Quarter Square 100,000 Large (fumar trees) 200,000 Medium (fumar trees). He noted that Tia didn't provide an overall estimate. PCBB – 'Possible Conflict Barnabas Brutus.' WFN – Work (and) Funding Needed.'

He climbed a flight of stairs to its base to an oaken entry. Inside, lay a circular chamber where a square-faced woman in the blue and gold tunic of the signal corps labored over a pile of papers.

The woman eyed him. "Sending or receiving?"

"Sending." He handed her the paper.

The clerk gave the slip a single glance. "You're in luck. It's a light day. We'll put it out in the next cycle. Should reach Equitant day after tomorrow." She counted the symbols, smiled, and said, "Two dinar and four bits for the message."

Two and a half dinars. A day's pay for a laborer. That didn't sound too bad.

"Forty-six towers at a half-dinar each, plus fees is twenty-six dinar and two bits."

Twenty-six dinar and change. A fortnights wages for a hard worker. Three good day's haul for a smith or wainwright. Such folk seldom used the towers. He'd sent messages three times via the network, the longest just twenty digits. Kyle reached into his pocket.

From the tower, Kyle took a steep, narrow road along the ridge into Stone Hollow proper, taking the curved streets past cottages and tenements to the business district. There, he stopped at the wainwrights. Yes, Miss Samos's coach was repaired. Yes, they could rent out a horse to pull it. And the cost? Well, just everything left of Tia's coin, save three coppers. Dratted woman must have an abacus between her ears.

Kyle entered the cheaper of Stone Hollow's two inns. This time of day, the place stood near empty, just him, the stout barkeep, and a pair of clerics hunched over bowls of stew.

He plopped his coins on the counter. "Food and a flagon of ale."

The barkeep eyed the offering. "Not enough."

Kyle flexed his fist.

"Bit early for ale," said a cracked female voice from behind him.

Dratted clerics. Always sticking their noses in other's business.

"Got anything else?" asked the innkeeper.

Kyle emptied his pockets. Two agates he'd found near the fumar trees, a candle stub, and Amelia's ring bounced onto the counter.

"Stones ain't worth spit." The innkeeper picked up the ring. "This might be worth something, though."

"No." The word escaped Kyle's lips with more force than he'd intended.

"Ah, a promise ring," said the priestess. "That's good."

The innkeeper eyed him. "Is Sister Miriam right? You getting hitched?"

"Yes." Kyle realized the word was true as it left his mouth.

"Fair enough." The innkeeper placed the ring back on the table. "Tell you what – I'll sell you yesterday's bread and cheese and put some thin ale in that skin for the coin on the table."

Weak ale beat water. "It'll do." Now that Kyle thought about it, driving back to Cosslet while buzzed probably wasn't a clever idea. Maybe that was why Amelia had given him water.

The clerics finished their meal. As they departed, the woman paused at his table and gave him a quizzical look. "You are a man of many talents. Losing them to drink would be an affront to God. Perhaps this will help guide you." She placed a token of Saint Fabia on the table.

Kyle started. Saint Fabia was the patroness of scholars, curiosity seekers, and wizards – not peasants or tradesmen. "You know?" He blurted the words without thinking even as he focused his Sight on the woman. Yes, an aura of arcane power clung to the priestess. Most clerics had no aptitude for sorcery. Then again, Fabia's clergy boasted more than their share of spellcasters. Strange, though. Fabia's order wasn't noticeably big and tended to stick to the cities. What was one doing out in the sticks? Traveling, maybe?

"I know you will make a good husband." With that, Sister Miriam exited the inn.

Amelia likes me. That thought stuck with him after he'd finished eating, hitched the carriage, and tossed the bike on its roof. Kyle chewed on that notion as he navigated the buggy along the Cosslet Road. Amelia liked him. His scars didn't faze her. She thought his magic was useful, not a demon sent curse. Her presence made the horrid visions and nightmares bearable.

More, the fumar trees and attendant work meant prosperity for the barony. It meant roads and canals and the businesses required to support those enterprises. He'd acquired a fair bit of grunt-level engineering expertise in the army. He could be part of that, maybe become a lockkeeper. Good, honest work.

Work. This job didn't pay squat. He'd taken it because of the completion bonus – well that and Tia's route would take him by his family's place. One hundred dinars, payable upon delivery of Tia Samos to Master Palo's offices in Corber Port. A tidy sum, enough to treat Amelia properly. But – was Tia still going to Corber Port?

EMPIRE: COUNTRY XIV – Peter

Weeks of scheming paid off. Mission accomplished. Nuptials loomed in Ian and Tia's future. Yet, Peter felt cheated, not satisfied.

Tia sat her cup on the dining table and faced Ian. "We need to discuss the forthcoming changes to Cosslet."

Ian smiled. "I would be pleased to show you my plans."

Peter watched as the pair rose from the table in unison and climbed the stairs arm in arm. They appeared compatible, what with their talk about trade regulations, taxes, and property management.

But, when Peter looked at Tia's face, he kept seeing Tessa. That disturbed him. He hadn't deserved Tessa during the war, and he wasn't worthy of her doppelganger now.

Ian suited Tia far better than Peter. He needed Tia to help run the barony. Which meant building the roads, canals, and camps needed to reach the Blight Wood – Peter's name for the fumar forest. That meant they'd be spending substantial time in Groveton.

Being apart from Tia and knowing she was happily married was tolerable. But the thought of Tia and Ian married, sharing a bed under his roof made Peter's gut burn. Maybe he could take up hunting. Harass Sigrid. Bust heads.

Peter rose and strode into the courtyard. Nothing moved. He kicked a stone. He walked to the castle gate, stared at Cosslet town. He tried to imagine it tripling in size, more shops, more people, more hustle, and bustle. Failed. It wouldn't be Cosslet anymore.

Peter turned from the gate and almost collided with Carter.

"Apologies, my lord."

"No need." Peter took in the guardsman, who wore a leather jerkin. A short old sword was belted to his waist. "Gate duty?"

"Yes, my lord."

Peter motioned at the deserted road. "Doesn't seem very busy."

"Usually, it's not," said Carter. "But now, with the bearak..."

"I understand." Peter nodded. "How about a sparring session?"

"But my duties – the gate"-

"Your duties require skill at arms. And those skills require honing." Peter motioned at the grassy patch where he'd drilled as a lad.

"Yes, my lord." Carter nodded; reluctance written across his face.

Shortly afterward, the courtyard rang with the 'thud' of wood against wood as the men tangled with practice blades.

Carter lasted exactly five strokes against Peter before being hurled onto his back.

"Up," Peter aimed his weapons wooden tip at the guardsman.

Carter managed a weak smile. "You're right, my lord. I've lost my edge since the war."

Peter watched Carter climbed to his feet. Ian's guardsman had never possessed much of an 'edge' to begin with. True, he'd been in the legions, but not in a front-rank cohort.

Carter assumed a fighter's crouch.

"Begin," said Peter.

Carter darted in and made a clumsy strike. Peter dodged and kicked the guardsman's legs out from underneath him. The guardsman rolled back towards Peter; blade angled skyward.

Pain exploded in Peters wrist. His wooden sword fell to the ground. "Tricky little cur!" Peter's boot lashed out and connected with his opponent's chin.

The guard fell back into the dirt.

Peter retrieved his weapon. "On your feet." He kicked the other sword towards Carter's hand.

Carter wiped blood from his face. "My lord, isn't this enough?"

"I said, on your feet!" Peter took a step towards the downed man. "Were I a pasty or a goblin, you'd be dead."

The guardsman nodded, took his sword, and rose, a bit unsteady on his feet.

"Begin," said Peter. Again, the two clashed. Carter, already shaky, lasted only two strikes before his blade spun away across the grass.

"Again," said Peter. This time the guard made a bull's rush that would have seen him impaled with real weapons.

Peter shook his head. Ian's lackey was no challenge at all.

"Again." This time Carter didn't charge, didn't move, just simply stood, and attempted the crude chops and stabs favored in the legions. Peter rewarded him with a bruised side and bashed head.

"Brother." Ian's voice came from behind Peter. "What are you doing?"

Peter turned to see his brother standing in the yard, Tia next to him, hands over her mouth. "Engaging in a spot of weapons practice with your man here."

"Practice?" Ian eyed Carter. The guardsman could barely stand. Blood and bruises covered his face. "This seems severe."

"War is a severe business," said Peter.

"The war ended two years past." Ian's glare made Peter feel like a child.

"It's alright, my lord." Carter took a wobbly step towards the dormitory. "I need the practice."

"No." Ian shook his head and pointed to the keep. "What you need is poultice and stitches. Have Bennett send Simon out; Lady Tia and I require him to drive our cart."

"Yes, my lord." Carter vanished inside the keep.

Peter turned to Ian. "Going somewhere?"

"I wish to investigate business opportunities." Tia's voice held no warmth whatsoever.

"And I offered to assist her." Ian placed an arm around Tia's shoulder.

"In that case," Peter threw his now-fractured practice sword across the yard, "I will accompany you, less the bearak make an appearance."

Tia grimaced. Ian's face hardened. "If you must."

"I must." Peter went to fetch his gear. Halfway up the stairs he encountered Simon Simpleton on the way down. He ducked into his room, donned a clean shirt, and descended to find the cart hitched, loaded, and trundling through the gate. Damn Ian. Was he trying to get his prospective wife killed?

Peter hastily donned his armor, grabbed his horse from the stable, turned, and almost collided with Father Barnabas.

"Is it true?" The priest practically hopped from foot to foot with excitement, head bobbing as he did so. "Is the Baron getting married?"

"It seems that way." Peter bulled past the priest.

"Ah, that is wondrous news. Too long has the shadow of loss hung over Ian."

Now it's hanging over me, thought Peter. "I must be after them."

"Of course," said Barnabas. "The Baron requires a guardian."

Peter grabbed the saddle and started to heave himself up.

The priest's eyes narrowed. "Are you remaining here?"

Peter paused. "I'm to be sheriff."

Barnabas nodded. "Ah, a fit trade for a warrior. I can offer council on the more mundane aspects of the job." He reached into his cassock. "Here, take this token of Mithras." His pudgy hand gripped a small sword and sun emblem. "A wandering priestess gave it to me last week."

"Thank you." A tiny jolt ran through Peter's hand when he grabbed the amulet. *I must have pricked myself.* He shoved it in his pocket and mounted. "I must be off. Good day."

Peter found the cart mired in a throng of farmers and petty tradesmen, each bent on a word with their Baron.

Peter pushed his horse into the crowd, who reluctantly parted ranks. "Make way! Stand aside!" Stupid peasants. Why did they have to be underfoot?

At length, Peter reached the wagon, where Ian spoke with a stout farmer in muddy breeches.

Ian gave him a disgusted look. "Peter, you're an ass."

"You left without me. That endangered Tia and yourself."

The farmer gave Peter an insolent glare and stomped to the roadside.

"There is no danger. The bearak has no doubt fled back into the forest."

Peter motioned at the peasants. "One of these louts might have a knife."

"They're my subjects. I know them. They're my friends."

More idiocy from Ian. "Like Sigrid is your friend? You know him as well. He sends men onto your lands to steal cattle, why not send one with a knife?"

Ian reeled back in shock. "Assassination is not Sigrid's style. Peter, must I ask you to leave the Barony again?"

Peter's body chilled in an instant. "We have an agreement." The words emerged through clenched teeth.

"And I will honor it, so long as you behave." Ian turned his attention to Tia.

"I shall."

They left the throng behind. Ian directed Simon to turn at a ramshackle house next to a huge weather-beaten barn in a field littered with junked wagons and unidentifiable detritus. Two barges rested on the riverbank, one of them black with rot.

Peter snorted. Cells place. He remembered John Cell from the Occupation. Cell fought when forced, but preferred scavenging battlefields and burned villages.

Peter brought his horse next to Ian. "Why call here? Cell is not the most reliable sort." Surely, Ian knew that.

"John Cell has...issues," said Ian, "but, he also has barges."

Peter motioned at the rotted watercraft. "Like that one?"

"Cell maintains other vessels," said Ian, "and associates along the river."

Associates? More like smugglers and criminals.

A massive cloth covered lump shifted as the cart entered the property. Six squat legs appeared beneath the gold and brown fabric, and a greenish gray tentacled snout appeared emerged from one end.

Simon halted the cart and stared at the beast with wide eyes. "What is that?"

"It's a droath." Peter realized Simon had probably never seen one of the beasts. "They're used to pull big wagons."

"Oh." Simon's gaze remained fixed on the creature. "I don't like it."

"It's harmless." Peter felt a hot spark against his chest.

"I believe that's Master Silam's beast," said Ian. "He's master of a troupe of entertainers, mostly gypsies."

Peter smiled. "I hope you have the fine silver locked away."

Heat burned against Peter's breastbone. What? He reached into his tunic and felt a warm lump – Kyle's pendant, the one that was supposed to provide warning of the bearak. Dratted stupid peasant and his stupid magic. He removed the amulet and jammed it in his saddlebag.

Two figures emerged from behind the droath, one with weathered features and ragged clothes, the other a muscular ebony-skinned man wearing a yellow robe with black spots.

Ian motioned at the pair. "Ah, there's Master Cell now. And Silam with him."

Simon helped Tia and Ian descend from the cart. Cell started walking in their direction while motioning at the house. Silam remained next to the droath.

Peter dismounted and began poking through the detritus – three wagon wheels with fractured rim's and broken spokes, half a dozen barrels that poked through the weeds like tree stumps, and a skeletal frame that might have been anything. Broken tools and rusted bits of metal filled the barn's interior. Junk, all of it. Surely, Tia could see that Cell was a poor business prospect.

Peter turned from the barn and almost collided with Silam.

"My apologies, good Knight." The black man made an elegant bow involving a bent knee, a swooping arm, and a pivot at the waist.

"I – uh – thank you," managed Peter. "I understand that's your droath?" He motioned at the beast, now pulling marsh weeds from the riverbank, and shoveling them into its maw.

Silam smiled. "Yes, that is my Regent there – Queen of the Southern Jungle. Usually, we make such a grand impression coming into a town such as this: her done up in fine blankets with hung with ribbons and bells, musicians before her and acrobats standing hand standing or tumbling atop the carts behind mine," his face fell, "but this time, alas, she is entering rut, my marvelous conveyance has a not so marvelous broken axle, and some of my performers quit the troop back at the coast." He sighed and continued. "I am considering resuming my travels via river barge while Regent spawns and those ham-handed workmen repair my axle, assuming I have any coin left for such."

"She must require a lot of upkeep."

"She does, she does," said Silam. "But her usefulness outweighs the cost. Speaking of which, I have preparations to undertake."

"The show."

"Yes, the show. I plan a most special performance tonight. Will you be there?"

A bit of frivolity might set matters right with Ian. "I believe so."

"Excellent." Silam bowed again, this time just a simple bending of the waist, and strode towards his droath. Regent wrapped a tentacle around his waist and lifted him onto her back. A moment later, the creature plunged down the riverbank and into the water, which barely reached to its knees.

A passing barge, piled high with cabbages, skirted the droath and its rider. Silam called out cheerful comments to its crew, who gaped as the beast scaled the far bank.

Peter blinked. Regent's gait seemed wrong, somehow, compared to the droath he remembered. The legs did not move in unison. Was it injured? If so, it did not affect the beasts speed as it ambled towards the forest. Perhaps the beast's pregnancy affected its stride. Yes, that sounded right.

"There you are."

Peter turned to find Ian and Tia behind him. "I was watching the droath."

Tia hung her head. "First Kyle and now you."

"What?"

"Kyle was obsessed with that smelly beast when we passed by here yesterday. Stopped the cart, dead in the road." Tia spun and made for the wagon.

Peter shook his head. "What got into her?"

Ian smiled. "John Cell. Tia wearied of his evasions and walked out."

She does have sense. Peter motioned at the cart. "Shall we depart?"

Ian assisted Tia onto the wagon before boarding himself. Simon flicked the reigns and steered the conveyance towards the road. Then he halted as Tia's coach appeared.

Naturally, Tia and Ian switched vehicles. Tia admonished Kyle to remain in uniform, a command the lout took in good cheer.

At the castle, Tia and Ian vanished into the keep.

Peter moped about the grounds, watching Simon and Kyle stable the horses. Amelia wandered over and wrapped herself around Kyle.

A rueful smile played across Peter's lips at the sight. No doubt a wedding loomed in their near future. Kyle might even be happy.

Peter doubted he would be happy at Groveton. Cosslet seemed constricting. Boring. Yes, exploiting the fumar trees required importing hundreds of laborers, but those would be just more peasants.

Bennet ducked into the courtyard long enough to claim Amelia.

Kyle busied himself fixing tack for Tia's horses, then strode about the yard, pausing now and again to eye the keep.

Peter approached him. "What's so interesting?"

"Huh?" Kyle's mouth dropped open.

"The keep, man. You keep staring at it."

"My lord, I – uh." Kyle took a breath and started over. "It needs fixing. The foundation is undermined." He pointed at the stonework. "See how the stones dip?"

Peter remembered Governor Rutherford's letter. He'd thought that a mere ploy, but Kyle had engineering experience, and if he agreed – "How bad?"

Kyle hesitated. "The army would order it torn down. My cohort did that twice. We replaced one with a watchtower. That took about a month."

Bennet appeared beside them. "Sir Peter, Baron Ian requests your presence in his study."

'Sir Peter.' Not 'Sir Peter Cortez,' no recognition for the bastard from the prim and proper Steward. Peter doubted that would change even after he became legitimized. Peter strode towards the keep without acknowledging the Stewards presence. Snubs worked both ways.

Ian perused papers as Peter entered the study. "We must make ready for the gala, so let's be quick." He shoved the papers across the desk.

Peter stared at the documents without sitting. "What are these?"

"What you asked for," said Ian. "Well, most of it." He removed the top sheet. "This is a request for expediency on your legitimization. It underlies the rest. I need your signature here." He pointed.

At last. Peter grabbed a quill and scrawled his name.

Ian handed Peter the second paper. "As per our agreement, this makes you the provisional Lord of Groveton."

"Provisional?" A tiny cold spot formed in Peter's gut. "Why?"

"Well, you must be legitimized, first. You must also learn what lordship entails – taxes and laws and settling disputes."

"Oh. Seems simple enough." Peter tried to imagine himself immersed in such trivia. It sounded dull as dirt.

"It's tedious." Ian motioned at a blank spot on the page. "Sign here."

Peter affixed his signature, more legibly this time.

Ian placed his hand across the remaining papers. "I can't appoint you sheriff."

"Why not?" The cold knot in Peter's gut grew. 'Sheriff' was the one position he was suited for in Cosslet. "Does this pertain to my legitimacy?"

"No." Ian seemed distraught. "Imperial law won't permit it."

"Imperial law?"

"I received this last year." Ian handed Peter another sheet, a formal imperial edict festooned with seals, signed by both Emperor Morgan DuSwaimair the Second and his cousin Solon. "It was issued in the wake of Lord Scarlet's rebellion."

"Oh." A chill entered Peter's bones. Jeremy Scarlet, the Red Knight, Left Hand of the Emperor – and a warrior turned rebel. Peter had been among his followers. He read the document. "... 'Judicial officials must be certified in law'... 'expertise in tariffs and road taxes'... what is this, brother? Where am I to attain these credentials?"

"Cato," said Ian. "Or Regis. Corber Port as well, should Tia continue her journey. The basic course requires three months."

Three months of his brains turning to mush from pouring over legal documents. *I'd sooner face the bearak armed with a kitchen knife. Or a demon.*

Ian presented the last sheet. "I can't appoint you Sheriff without drawing Imperial ire upon my house. However, I can appoint you Constable."

Constable. A position fit for peasants. Peter's face fell.

Ian reached across the table with concern written on his face. "Peter, it's the best I can do."

Peter stared at the sheet. "I'll think about it."

Ian exhaled. "Do so. We must make ready." He gathered the papers together. "Wear your best."

"I shall." Peter exited the study feeling dazed.

Peter donned his 'best suit.' First a pair of vertically striped gray and white pantaloons. A frilly white shirt covered his torso, but two frills were missing, and the side was ripped. Fortunately, his dark jacket would cover that defect, though it sported a patched elbow and a cut hem. A worn wig and a broad hat with a bedraggled feather completed the ensemble. When he stared in the mirror, an impoverished genteel aristocrat stared back. Peter considered the reflection, remembering the times he'd been mocked as 'Sir Pauper' and 'Beggar Knight.' He shook his head at the recollections. He was a warrior. Playing dress-up was silly. But sometimes frippery was called for. A bright object caught his eye: the pendant of Saint Mithras given him by the priest. He hefted the talisman. It suited him. He draped the relic about his neck and strode from the room.

The others waited downstairs, dressed in their best. Bennet wore a formal scribe's tunic complete with vest, while Marta had exchanged her apron for a pink dress with a cream top.

Ian wore green breeches, worn coat, and a peaked hat.

Tia was drop dead gorgeous, hair done in a flowing style that only seemed casual, slim body wrapped in a blue and silver gown that accented her curves.

Peter's breath caught. Tessa wore a similar outfit during formal occasions in the camps. They looked so much alike. But Tia had eyes only for Ian.

"You can afford this?" Tia gazed into Ian's eyes; her fingers intertwined with his.

"Oh, I have coins set aside." Ian's voice held a jovial note.

Hot anger built within Peter at the sight. He reached reflexively for his sword hilt.

"Peter," called Ian. "Glad you could make it."

"Likewise," Peter managed a stiff nod. "I'm not used to these clothes."

"Well, get used to them," said Ian. "They come with the job."

'If you say so." Peter eyed Tia. He couldn't stand to see them together. Cosslet held no appeal. He'd leave, make his way in another part of the Empire. But not tonight. Tonight he'd at least pretend to happiness.

"Let's go!" Celina skipped to the door, clad in a bright pink dress.

The others followed her into the courtyard, where Kyle loomed alongside the carriage. Somehow, the oaf looked presentable despite his grotesque scar and too-small jacket. Maybe he'd bathed.

They boarded the coach one by one. Then Kyle shut the door, climbed to the driver's bench, and flicked the reigns.

Silam's droath towed a train of brightly painted wagons into the market square as Kyle parked the coach before the inn.

Peter spotted Rebecca and another gypsy woman engaged in a discordant musical duet atop one cart while a sultry wench swayed to the rhythm. A juggler strode along the wagon tops, perpetually one misstep or catch from catastrophe, yet he neither plummeted nor missed a throw.

"I wonder what's in the wagons?" asked Celina.

"Their contents will be revealed after the performance," said Silam's distinctive voice from behind them.

Peter, Tia, and Ian turned as one to see the ebony entertainer standing near the door. Silam' gaze fixed Ian. "Special accommodations have been prepared for your party, my lord Cortez." He made another of his elaborate bows. "My assistant will escort you." A brightly clad gypsy appeared alongside his master and guided them into the inn.

EMPIRE: COUNTRY XV – Tia

The air inside the inn had a sweet aroma to it. Faint silvery mist distorted the lamps glow. Tia had the impression of walking through an underwater grotto. "This way, this way," urged their handsome gypsy guide. He guided the Baron's party to a row of comfortable chairs set behind a table covered with a white cloth.

"Thank you," said Ian.

The gypsy made an elaborate bow. "Only the best for the Baron. If you will excuse me"-

Ian waved his hand. "Of course."

Tia took in the chamber, spotting semi-familiar faces from both Cosslet and Lupton. Crowds packed seats where the table had been. Jason Vasquez chatted with a farmer from Lupton, while his children made faces at Anatoly's offspring. Scores of laborers filled long benches along the wall. Tia placed the crowd at over four hundred. The only vacant area was a makeshift stage dominated by a huge puppet theater.

A colorfully clad gypsy woman dropped off pastries and fizzy drinks at Ian's table before vanishing back into the throng in a swirl of skirts.

Ian hefted one of the beverages and took a sip. His right eyebrow rose. "Not bad."

Peter grabbed a glass and downed it in a single gulp without a word. Tension radiated from his lanky frame in waves. Tia remembered the way he'd beaten Ian's guardsman black and blue and the cold glances he'd cast at Ian. Jealous. And prone to fits of anger. Not a good combination. She'd have to address that.

A gypsy escorted an impassive Consul Sigrid and a scowling Steward Kessler to a nearby table. Sigrid wore a worn formal toga. Kessler's garb matched Bennet's.

Ian leaned towards the Consul. "Welcome."

Sigrid acknowledged the greeting with a glance.

Celina tugged Sigrid's toga. "Where's Liam?"

The Consul stared down his nose at her. "Liam is ill. My cousin Andric tends to him."

Ian placed a tiny cup in Tia's hand. Tingles shot through her body at the first sip. "I don't recognize the vintage." That puzzled Tia: she'd imbibed alcoholic concoctions aplenty at Solace, a city famous for its wines.

"Nor do I." Ian placed his hand atop hers.

Another thrill ran through Tia's body, combined with a cascade of lightning-quick thoughts: 'He's cute, and he's mine.' 'What will our children look like?' 'Is he any good in bed?' That thought made her giggle, prompting a sly look from the Baron. 'I can teach him a thing or two in that department.' Another unadvertised benefit of her university years.

A bright red light flashed on the stage, accompanied by a puff of smoke. When the haze cleared, Silam stood before the puppet box with outstretched hands, clad in his leopard fur cape and a white kilt. Gold rings set with red gems dangled from his ears, and more gold adorned his wrists and fingers. A blue on black tattoo of a fanged creature was barely visible on his chest.

The magician bowed. Tiny pink, violet, and silver balls dropped from his cape. The wizard made a fumbling effort to catch the orbs, which morphed into a juggling display. After three or four passes, he inhaled a great gulp of air – along with the spheres.

Silam's face assumed a pained expression as he rubbed his belly. A moment later a long tongue of fire shot from his mouth. The flame transformed into a fiery serpent with tiny wings that darted about the chamber.

A gasp escaped Tia as this apparition passed overhead before diving into a round glass jar at the wizard's feet. An intense orange glow came from this container.

Shadows flickered and danced on the wall behind Silam assuming animalist shapes. The audience gasped when these phantasms stepped from the wall and prowled about the sorcerer; strange things like ink black cats and lizards that went from being the size of mice one moment to nearly as large as horses the next. Silam seemed more cross than frightened by these apparitions; finally leaning over them and saying words in a heathen tongue which caused not only the shadow creatures to vanish, but his own shadow as well. "That wasn't supposed to happen." A puzzled expression appeared on the conjurer's face. "If I have no shadow, then I cannot be here," and with that he vanished in a puff of smoke which grew larger and larger even as it thinned away to nothing, to reveal a pair of slim, fit gypsy girls in tight pink leotards.

Eerie flute and string music commenced, and the girls began a series of moves that was as much dance as it was gymnastics. They swirled, they leapt, they juggled – a series of moves that ended with the girls linking hands, and a twisting move that had the one girl standing on the inn floor, hands up and linked to the other girl who was looking down. They dropped in a twisting fall, and the room descended into darkness.

The puppet booth lit up, and the music took on a random tone. The curtains swept aside on the miniature theater, revealing a scene of nobles at court. These figures began a whirling dance, causing their finery to shift and exposing rags underneath – and then the dancers were peasants carousing in a wooded clearing.

A new figure appeared, this one a holy knight carrying a gleaming sword. "I seek the lost princess."

"Go there! No, there! This way! That way!" The peasants pointed in a different direction with each word.

"Ah, I see." The knight blundered into the forest while the dancers twirled once more.

The scene shifted to a princess in a pointed hat and gauzy veil arguing with a bear. At length, the bear had enough and leaped upon the princess, sending her pointed hat flying. Tia screamed in concert with the rest of the audience.

The mist about the stage thickened and turned pink, shot through with violet strands. A cloying scent filled the air.

On stage, the puppet knight appeared and swore fealty to a puppet bandit. *That's not right.*

Sharp, stabbing pain erupted behind Tia's eyes. She blinked and rubbed her head.

Now the puppet knight strode into the noble court. "I don't see my daughter," said the monarch from his throne. "Why have you returned?"

"To bring true justice." The puppet knight swung his sword, and blood erupted from the stump of the king's neck.

Wrong! Outrage at the renegade knight's act burned in Tia's chest. Her dismay, though, emerged as a strangled squawk.

"No." Peter's chair clattered to the floor as he stood.

Behind Tia, Kyle's voice rang out, muttering a mystical incantation that raised the hairs on her arms.

But on stage, the wooden massacre continued as the knight executed every member of the court.

Tia attempted to speak, to voice outrage, but couldn't. What was happening?

Then the pink mist filled Tia's vision, and everything changed.

EMPIRE: COUNTRY XVI – Peter

Peter 'oohed' and 'awed' with the rest of the crowd at Silam's phantasmal beasts and convoluted illusions. But, what riveted his attention, though was the puppet theater. The miniature warrior's circumstances resonated with Peter – ordered about by incompetent buffoons, cheated by sly peasants, and protracted periods of pointless, aimless riding. Peter understood the Puppet Knight's spiral into darkness because he'd lived it on the brutal battlefields of Drakkar and Kitrin. Echoes of past slaughter's appeared in his mind's eye as the tale progressed and the inn's lights faded to near extinction. Shadows played suggestively along the wall: a beast, a sword, a noose, each heightening the tension.

Peter blinked at a droning sound behind him – wait, that was Kyle, mouthing an incantation. But why? Peter rotated his head, an act requiring immense exertion. Something sinuous brushed against his hat. Peter tilted his neck upward and spied a purplish tendril dangling from the pinkish mass clinging to the ceiling. He blinked again, and spotted hundreds of identical appendages, all descending towards the heads of the enraptured audience. "No!" The word emerged from his parched throat as a choked gasp.

A faint aura clung to Kyle, who sat motionless on his bench.

It's a trap. "No." Peter struggled to his feet. His chair clattered to the floor.

On stage, the Puppet Knight massacred the king's court.

Tia sighed. Her head hit the table with a tendril buried in her neck.

Peter made to sever it, but his arm felt sluggish. Sharp pain pierced the back of his skull. He couldn't stand. And then he fell into a dead red wasteland.

PETER RODE AMONG A column of knights traversing a crumbling road through a wasteland of reddish-brown hills. A cold thrill ran through Peter's body. He knew this land. Drakkar. A realm of war without end. A major theater of the Traag War.

Another knight pulled his horse beside Peter. "True God above, but I loathe this wretched country."

Peter stared at the speaker; features contorted in shock. Sir Leroy. This can't be real. He slapped his mounts neck. Contact. He inhaled acrid red dust laced with sweat.

Leroy persisted. "I swear this land is accursed. Why are we here? Let the wretched pasties murder each other, I say."

"We are here to slaughter the Empire's enemies." Sir Benedict spoke from behind Sir Leroy.

That wasn't right. Yes, they were warriors, but...Peter couldn't think.

Sir Leroy, though, nodded in agreement. "Kill them before they kill us."

As if to punctuate his words, a short creature leaped from a concealed pit right in front of the knight, waving a notched blade and bleating a battle cry from its elongated snout which sounded much like a squealing pig. Dirt fell from the things hide, exposing green-gray skin.

Goblins, thought Peter, even as he reached for the blade at his side. His mind registered more eruptions from either side. Something slammed into his armor and skittered into the dirt. An arrow, one of hundreds falling from the sky.

Ahead of Peter, goblins swarmed out of the dirt and climbed the steeds of the knights before him.

Peter kicked at one green-skinned wretch and cleaved the skull of another with his sword.

One horse reared, hurling its rider to the ground where the green-skinned vermin piled atop him. Another horse toppled sideways, pinning its rider.

"There're hundreds of the beggars!" Peter recognized Sir Gregory's voice.

Sir Benedict raised his sword with a gauntleted hand. "Ambush! Ride and reform!"

A squat knight with a bushy beard galloped past Peter wielding an enormous double-bladed ax. Sir Damon Hard. Behind him, screaming like a madman was another familiar visage: Sir Randolph Fury. The pair plowed right through a knot of goblins, leaving orange blood and dismembered bodies in their wake.

Peter took advantage of the opening and charged after them.

A mile later, the company paused to take stock.

"Five!" Sir Benedict raised his hand. "Five good knights murdered by that filth."

"We'll make them pay." Sir Leroy swayed in his saddle as he spoke the words. A purple bruise covered half his face and a nasty gash across his sword arm.

Leroy wasn't the only wounded man amongst the dozen survivors. Sir Manfred slumped in his saddle. Squire Rock's face was pasty white, and his breath came in shallow gasps.

"You require healing." Sir Gregory steadied Leroy. "So, do they." He motioned at Sir Manfred, whose lifeblood dripped from his armor and Squire Rock, who clenched his left arm in a death grip.

"There." Peter pointed at a rude clutch of huts clinging to a nearby hillock.

Sir Bear gave the hamlet a suspicious glance. "Pasty place. Murder us in our sleep, like as not." He spat on the ground.

"It will suffice," said Sir Benedict.

"Perhaps it has a tavern," said Sir Leroy through his grimace.

Sir Hard and a couple of the other Knights guffawed at the remark. Pasties preferred narcotic powders and mists to alcohol. Taverns were almost unheard-of outside imperial enclaves.

The hamlet boasted a hundred thin, pale wretches ranging from four to forty winters in age, dwelling in a score of huts encircled by a half-collapsed wall that dated to an earlier era.

"You're out of luck." Sir Hard patted Leroy on the back. "No tavern."

"Or anything else," said Sir Gregory. "No shops, just the well and one of those wretched heathen shrines." He indicated a flat stone flanked by carved posts wrapped with strips of colored cloth.

None of the peasants looked their visitors in the eye. None admitted to speaking the imperial tongue.

Sir Benedict dismounted, grabbed a wretch by his shirtfront, and pointed at the largest hovel. When the peasant responded with gibberish, the Knight-Commander gave the lout a backhanded blow that knocked him clear off his feet. "One must be firm with these animals."

The sensation of wrongness returned to Peter. Benedict was an ass, but not needlessly brutal. But brutality suited Drakkar. Its despots reveled in their cruelty, mutilating, and murdering their subjects at the slightest whim.

But right or not, the villagers received the Knight-Commanders message: they vacated the hut and brought out a bundle of dead grass for the horses.

The knights assisted their wounded comrades into the cottage, a square thing with one room, two windows, and a loft. Sir Fury motioned at a row of dirty straw pallets. "Filthy place. It should be burned."

Stout, black haired Sir Manfred was the worst injured of the lot, having taken first a dagger and then an arrow through his right leg. Squire Bookman, who boasted a year of medical study in far off Solace, shook his head. "He may lose the leg without a proper healer."

Next, the learned squire turned his attention to ruddy-faced Squire Rock. The lad sported a deep gash across his ribs and side. "The lung wasn't punctured," he said. "Salve, broth and a good night's sleep should serve him."

The squire shook his head at Sir Leroy. "The swelling is superficial."

"Hah!" Sir Leroy spat.

Squire Bookman ignored the outburst. "His arm troubles me. I can splint it, but this requires a true healer's expertise."

Sir Benedict addressed the company. "We need intelligence of the enemy's whereabouts and our best route from this place. I shall take half the company to a vantage point I glimpsed earlier to judge the lay of the land."

The commander's statement prompted more mutters as the men debated which was worse – blundering into another green-skin ambush, or remaining in this dead, dull place with the treacherous locals?

Peter elected to join Benedict. Sir Fury declared he'd go mad if left in the hamlet, and Sir Hard said he'd sooner hunt goblins than kill ghosties. Gregory wavered – Bookman was his friend – but mounted his horse at the last moment.

They sat out into the crisp dawn air. "I see a trail." Sir Fury pointed at a flat strip of dirt that veered into the hills.

The Knights followed the track past a field where the villagers tended rows of wilted plants. From there, it entered a gorge between steep slopes littered with sharp shards.

Gregory pointed at a dark spot above them. "It's an old mine."

"Search it," said the commander. The knights nodded in agreement. Goblins often made their homes in such shafts.

Peter and Gregory scaled the slope. A ring of fire-blackened stones marked the entry. They struck torches and entered a dark tunnel supported with rotten timbers that ended amidst fallen rubble. Broken tools and bits of wood dotted the floor.

"Empty," Peter told the Commander. "No greenskin's."

"A played-out pit, like Drakkar's other mines," said Gregory.

They followed the track deeper into the hills, encountering no traffic save a pair of terrified shepherds who fell to their faces and bleated incoherent pleas that sounded little different from their charges.

Twice more, the Commander sent men into cramped mines. Another time, they investigated a tangle of fallen masonry, a manor from a past era. Damon Hard pulled a bent spoon from the heap, eyed it critically, and threw it away.

The Knights mounted their steeds and followed the path to a tall hill capped with a waist-high ring of stones, the remnant of a fort or watch post. Sir Gregory produced his spyglass and surveyed the terrain.

"There. That must be Fort Salamander." He handed the glass to Benedict, who peered at the distant formation.

"We'll try for it tomorrow," said Sir Benedict. "I make the distance at ten, perhaps twelve miles from our current glorious accommodations."

They began the return journey.

Peter wiped his brow upon exiting the cleft. Before him, the ground fell to the dismal plot of cropland. His throat felt dry as dust. He looked forward to slaking his thirst.

Sir Fury's hand descended on Peter's shoulder. "Somethings wrong."

"What?" Then Peter saw it – no peasants moved among the plants. No smoke rose from the huts.

"The pasties did a runner," said Hard.

"Or they're hiding." Gregory turned in his saddle as he spoke the words.

"Perhaps the goblins attacked," said Peter.

"Weapons at the ready." The air filled with the hiss of metal sliding against leather as the Knights unsheathed their swords.

They charged at the hamlet's wall, horses leaping over the barrier as though it weren't there. Then they halted. Nothing moved in the yard apart from a solitary dog. No villagers. No knights. No horses.

Peter's gut turned to ice as he rotated his horse in a circle. Every shadow concealed a foe.

Sir Benedict leaped from his mount. Peter followed him to the hut where they'd left the wounded. Flies buzzed about the entry.

"God above, no!" Squire Bookman was speared to the far wall. Leroy's head glared at them from the floor, crudely hacked from his body, which still rested on the table. Squire Rock slumped in a chair, a red smile across his neck.

Benedict whirled. "Four men remain missing. Search this dung heap."

Peter joined the others in poking through the huts. Sir Hard found two members of the company in one hovel, their bodies riven with stab wounds.

Bear found a third in the compound's corner with goblin arrows protruding from his back. "He tried to run, didn't make it," said the Knight.

A call brought Peter to a cottage beside the one they'd claimed. There, Gregory crouched next to a tilted stone with a dark void behind it. "A tunnel." He pointed at marks in the dirt. "Goblins. They were working together."

The Knights reported their discoveries to Sir Benedict, who stood in the first hut, staring at Sir Leroy's severed head. "Find them."

The villager's trail wasn't hard to follow. It led to the defunct mine they'd scouted earlier.

Sir Hard eyed the entrance. "Close quarters in there."

"We're not going in." Sir Benedict pointed at Peter and Gregory. "Gather brush. We're smoking them out."

Smoke billowed from the cave, along with sooty, choking ghosties. The Knights forced them to the ground, executing those who tried to flee. Then they entered the noxious tunnel and dragged out the remainder, oldsters, women, and children, whom they propped against the cliff.

Sir Benedict yanked an older man to his feet. "What happened?"

The villagers quailed. Women and children huddled against the back wall. The oldest stepped forward. "Many goblin come," he said. "Want kill, you, or us. Say go. We go."

"*You turned coat.*"

"*Want live.*"

"*Not anymore.*" The Commander waved at his troops. "*Kill them all.*" Screams and pleas filled the air.

Peter advanced with the rest. His sword sank into the gut of a screaming woman who spat blood and died. Then he cleaved the skull of a child who threw himself at his legs. He stabbed one man in the throat and broke the head of another with his gauntlet.

Beside him, Gregory speared a screaming child through the back while Damon Hard decapitated his mother and Sir Fury twisted a man's neck like it was a chicken.

Then the screaming stopped. Peter stepped back from the cliff, armor covered in blood, eyes wide in horror. The villagers were dead. All of them.

"We did what was right and proper. We gave the empires enemies the deaths they so richly deserved." Sir Benedict faced Peter with a feral smile plastered across his face. "There is a beast within us all. Today, yours was unleashed."

Why is Benedict saying these things? Peter eyed the mound of corpses. "I'd prefer mine remained caged."

"Bah!" Benedict grabbed Peter's shoulder and gave him a hard shove. "You enjoy dealing death, watching life-sparks fade from those you kill. I see it in your eyes."

"No!" Peter tried to pull away from the Commander, but Benedict's fingers were like iron claws. "I fight for the Empire, not for bloodlust."

"One does not preclude the other." Benedict's eyes flashed red as he spoke.

"No!" Peter tore his arm free. His fist lashed out and connected squarely with Benedict's nose. And for the first time since awakening in this nightmare, he felt right. Justified.

Sir Benedict's body struck the ground.

Peter stood over him. "You are not Sir Benedict DuPaul."

The Knight commander eyed him from the ground. "You're right," he said in a raspy voice. Then he vanished.

Peter blinked. The other Knights were gone, along with the villager's corpses. He stood alone at the base of a steep slope covered in broken rock.

"What – What happened?" Old memories warred with his recent experiences. "Where'd they go?"

"Your companions were never present." The whisper drifted from the overhead rocks.

"Who are you?" Peter scrambled along the cliff, searching for a way up.

"You bear my talisman. But are you worthy of it?"

"What are you talking about?" Peter found a rising gully that offered multiple handholds.

"Salvation," said the whisper. "The demon was correct. Bloodlust stains your soul. What was done cannot be undone. Yet, atonement is possible."

"Demon?" Peter reached the gully's top and pulled himself onto a wide ledge. Past it, a fractured wall offered handholds.

"Demons take many things. This one took your memory and twisted it." The voice was close, now just yards above his head.

Peter ascended another foot. "I don't understand."

"Tell me, what did Sir Benedict say after the massacre?"

Peter stopped, his hand on a protruding knob. He thought back to that horrible day. "He said it was 'necessary' and that was it." He raised his foot and stuck it in a crevice.

"Did you fight him?"

"No." Peter heaved himself up the cliff. "I was ashamed."

"Because you realized what was necessary was also wrong." The voice was close now.

One last heave. Peter extended his hand to the overhead ledge and pulled. His arm muscles burned. Something sharp dug into his chest.

Peter stared at an old warrior in bronze armor of ancient design, the breastplate dominated by the image of a stylized bull. A white-bearded face, pleasant to look on, peeped through a winged helmet. That face radiated trust, confidence, and determination. That face looked familiar.

I've seen him before. But where? *An image appeared in Peter's mind of an old knight who wandered through the war camps dispensing encouragement and advice.* What was his name? Sir Matthew? No, that wasn't it. Something like that though. Sir Mattes. Yes. That was it. Sir Mattes of Sunstone. But what was he doing in this...whatever it was?

"*You found me,*" *said the armored oldster.*

"*Found?*" *It hurt to speak.* "*Who are you?*"

The oldster's response was a small sad smile. "*I stand against the dark,*" *he said at last, though in truth he looked barely capable of standing at all. A bronze sword lay across his lap, its blade covered in tiny runes.*

"*Can you help me?*"

"*You bear my talisman.*" *The oldster adjusted his position. The sword in his lap shifted towards Peter.* "*Now take my blade. They go together, one into the other.*"

Peter reached out and felt cool metal.

PETER'S EYES FLICKED open. He was in a red lit room of wood, the light coming from glowing reddish something attached to the ceiling – something that looked part pillow, part cloud, part spider, and all menace. He was half sitting, half lying on uncomfortable wooden things. His wrists were bound together even further to the side, hard up against something sharp and painful.

Chants and discordant music came from outside the room.

Peter blinked. The wooden shapes resolved themselves into puppets. That ornate cloth belonged to the puppet monarch. A patch of rough fur went with the bear. And the metal plates were part of the puppet knight's armor.

Kyle's immense bulk sprawled beside him. Peter elbowed the oaf. His breathing didn't change.

Then came a scream of terror and agony that chilled his blood. Somebody had just been murdered.

Frantic, Peter twisted his body. Then he realized his right hand clenched something: the hand and hilt of the puppet knight's sword. "Take my sword," he whispered.

He pulled. The miniature weapon pulled free of the knight. But how? Wasn't it part of the puppet?

"These are the last ones." The voice was rustic, earthy.

"Good." A sigh accompanied the word. "I'm beat."

The wall split apart.

Peter stared at a short man in dark woolen clothing. Behind him was a taller person in leather armor.

"Hey, he's awake."

Peter moved. He swiveled with the knife's hilt clenched in both hands. And bronze blades tip slid between the speaker's ribs.

The speaker fell to his knees. Blood bubbled from his lips.

His companion took a step back, hand already reaching for the sword at his side.

Peter didn't give him a chance to draw it. He kicked, hurling himself through the opening, knocking the leather clad man reeling. Then he was on the ground, spitting out dirt.

Peter flipped himself onto his back. He needed to free his hands.

Too late. The warrior in leather loomed above him, sword raised.

EMPIRE: COUNTRY XVII - Kyle

Silam's sorcery far surpassed Kyle's. That was apparent at their first encounter and blatantly obvious when the Saban got onstage.

Then again, Kyle wasn't much of a magician, not anymore. He'd felt his powers erode away bit by bit for months now. Too much drink and not enough study.

Mystic powers pulsed with each change of scene during the play, fanning out over the audience, enhancing the performance. Kyle shifted in his seat. Street-corner conjurers occasionally employed similar magics to entice coins from their spectators, but not on this scale. This was beyond the ability all but a the strongest of Solace's master magicians. The sorcery in the room continued to build. A headache built behind his eyes. This wasn't a performance. It was something else. He reflexively mouthed the words to a protective spell. Too little, too late.

Darkness.

"WHY DO WE EVEN BOTHER with these dullards?" The cultured, aristocratic voice came from beside Kyle. *"Not one of them possesses significant talent."*

Pale witch-light appeared, illuminating a slender man with curly black hair in the robe of a master sorcerer, silver sigils against a blue surface.

"Master Antigonus!"

"Speak when spoken to, dolt." Master Antigonus finished the statement with a theatrical sigh.

Another figure in the robe of a master sorcerer emerged from the shadows: a tall, long-faced man with brown hair. Kyle recognized him as well: Master Lysander.

Antigonus squinted at Kyle, then glanced at Lysander. "I observe no arcane aura about this one. Are we sure he's even a novice? Mayhap he's a laborer playing charades."

Novice? Kyle flicked his eyes downward. Yes, he wore the white robe of a novice magician instead of the ridiculous driver's outfit. What happened? Had he dreamed the last few years? Drank himself into madness?

"He's a novice, all right," said Lysander. "Talented in fire charms and location, with potential in fixing, and perhaps"-

"Spare me." Antigonus fixed his gaze on Kyle. "Come with us, novice." He entered a rocky tunnel without waiting for a response.

Kyle followed the masters, mind reeling in confusion. Novice? He'd passed his novice trials years ago. But sure enough, the master's led him to a black portal he remembered extremely well. And what was this dull, cold pain in his wrist?

Antigonus pressed a bit of wax into his hand. "Find the candle." He turned to Lysander. "Care to wager a copper bit should he fail?"

Lysander grunted.

Kyle focused his mind. This should be simple. Location spells – finding – came easily to him. He worked the spell and let out a grunt as hot needles of pain bored his wrist. Features contorted, Kyle tried the spell a second time – and again the charm failed. Frustrated, he jabbed a meaty arm into the darkness. "There."

"Not even close." Antigonus shook his head. "I should mark you down for cheating."

Antigonus waved an arm, and witch-light shined into the dark chamber, revealing a clutter of boxes, chairs, and trinkets. The candle perched atop a rickety table. "You're a miserable failure at location spells. Let's see about your vaunted ability with fire. Ignite the candle."

Kyle cleared his mind. Concentrated. He envisioned the wick bursting into flame – but the only fire was in his forearm. "Something is wrong."

"Silence, novice." The master's eyes assumed a reddish tinge as he glared at Kyle. "The only thing 'wrong' is the selection process that admitted a talentless oaf like you into the novice ranks."

"We still have other tests to conduct," said Lysander.

"Waste of time." Antigonus shook his head.

"I insist." Lysander entered the room and lifted the pieces of a broken clay mug. "Novice Kyle displayed talent at mending spells."

"Oh, very well." Antigonus motioned at Kyle. "Go fix the cup, peasant."

Kyle failed that test. And the next. And the one after that. A sense of wrongness grew in him with each failure. And each time, invisible hot needles stabbed his wrist. This shouldn't be happening.

Finally, Antigonus called a halt. "Novice Kyle, you are a no-talent oaf without a place in the Arcane Cohorts." He pointed at a distant door. "I remand you back to the legions."

Numb and defeated, Kyle plodded towards the door. How had he failed so miserably? Fire and Finding came effortlessly to him. Fixing required concentration but was still within his capabilities. What happened in there? Frustrated, he banged his hand into the stone wall – and stopped at the sound of a tiny 'clang.'

"Well, well, if it isn't my favorite loafer," said a familiar, despised voice from just outside the tunnel.

Kyle eyed the swarthy man just past the entry. Centurion Stilicho, cruelty incarnate and given a legion uniform. Kyle's personal bane for the three years he'd been in the ranks.

A gap-toothed smile appeared on Stilicho's face. "Always knew you were gaming the army with that magic crap." The centurion flicked his wrist, and a coiled whip studded with metal and glass appeared in his hand. "I figure you need punishing."

Stilicho's eyes flared red as the whip hissed and cracked.

Cloth tore, and pain flared where the barbs struck Kyle's shoulder.

Kyle ignored the pain and continued to walk towards the centurion. Red eyes.

Antigonus's eyes had flashed crimson back in the tunnels. And Antigonus, while an aristocratic asshole, wasn't a cruel man.

The whip bit into Kyle's hide a second time.

He stepped past the door, on a stone paved path cut into a steep grassy slope dotted with cottages – the south face of Mystic Mountain, where the Arcane Cohorts trained in the magical arts.

"I forgot how tough you were." Stilicho's red-tinted eyes bored into Kyle. "Gave you fifty lashes once, and you just shrugged it off."

Kyle ignored the comment and took another step. One more, and he'd be within reach of the centurion. Two more and they'd collide.

"Halt, trooper!"

Kyle took another step and grabbed Stilicho's arm. It felt hot and greasy, not human at all.

"Unhand me!" Stilicho's free hand slammed into Kyle's gut. "I'll have you executed for disobedience!"

"No, you won't." Kyle forced Stilicho's hand towards his wrist. He understood what the pain was, why he'd failed, and what confronted him.

It was a Null Rune, attached to his wrist. It leached his power each time he'd tried casting a spell. He couldn't overcome a Null Rune – no mortal could – but demons were arcane power incarnate.

"You can't do this," screamed Stilicho. "You have no power!"

"I have strength." Stilicho's hand contacted the ring of pain gripping Kyle's wrist.

The centurion's body jerked. His features contorted and melted.

White-hot agony shot through Kyle's wrist, making him stagger. Tears of pain came through his eyes. But he didn't release his grip on the demon.

The Stilicho demon imploded.

KYLE OPENED HIS EYES as a something round and metallic 'clanged' off the floor. He wasn't at Mystic Mountain anymore. Instead, he was in a wooden room, sprawled atop a collection of wooden objects that dug into his back and sides. Weird music, high pitched sounds, and unintelligible voices reached his ears. Thick cords bound his wrists and ankles. None of that mattered. His power was back.

Kyle stood, balancing on bound feet. He spotted Peter on the ground outside the room. A dark-haired man in leather armor stepped before the Knight, sword raised.

No time to hesitate. Kyle knelt and grabbed one of the wooden things he'd been reclining on, leaped, and swung.

The swordsman's face turned as Kyle fell. His eyes widened. He took a step back – and then the puppet Kyle clenched slammed into his skull. Bone and brains flew.

Twigs whipped into Kyle's face as he slammed into the ground. He raised his head and spat dirt and grass.

"The big ones loose!" The voice came from an aisle between dense shrubbery and the parked wagons.

Light glinted off metal near Kyle's nose – the sword of the man he'd killed. He ran his bound wrists along the edge. The bonds severed. A second swipe freed his legs.

Three men appeared, each wearing leather armor and carrying naked steel.

"They're all awake." A shock of yellow hair topped the speaker's head. "Regent will be here."

"There he is!" A swarthy man pointed right at him.

Kyle rose to a crouch.

A blade just missed his skull.

"Take him!"

The speaker was in front of him. A distraction. Kyle stabbed backward. The sword tip bit into something soft.

"Augh!" The blond man stumbled into Kyle's peripheral vision, clenching his side.

Three on one. Not good odds. Kyle possessed competence with a blade but wasn't a master swordsman. However, he had other talents. Kyle focused on the swarthy one and unleashed his fire spell.

Multicolored sparks played across the swarthy man's body. "Hah! The Masters magic protects me." Then he collapsed, blood pouring from his mouth.

Peter stepped into view, red-stained sword in hand.

Moments later, the bandit's companions joined him in death.

Peter approached Kyle, face set in stone. "We must spar more often. Your blade work is sloppy."

Numbly, Kyle nodded.

Peter knelt, pulled one knife from the dead man's belt and a second from his boot. He handed one to Kyle, who numbly accepted it.

A godawful shriek, the last terrified sound of a dying woman, rose above the bizarre piping music. The hairs on Kyle's neck and arms rose. A tingling sensation rushed through his body. Dark magic was being worked here.

Peter's head jerked erect. "Tia!" He ducked his head inside the wagon beside the corpses. "Empty." He strode towards the source of the racket. "Follow me."

Kyle took a breath. Tia. Of course, the fool Knight would try to rescue a woman he barely knew. A woman. Amelia. She was here, too. Kyle grunted. His face contorted. Then he set out after Peter. Highborn weren't the only fools.

EMPIRE: COUNTRY XVIII – Tia

Tia checked her dress in the mirror. Perfect. No. That ruffle was out of place. And what happened to the hem? Would Ian notice? She bit her lip. Probably not. Men, in her experience, cared little about fashion. But the other women most certainly would spot the imperfections. The bitches would gossip about minute flaws for weeks.

True God above, this dress was horrible. It was almost half Tia's weight, chaffed at the waist and a needle or errant knot of fabric dug into her skull's base. It felt like an immense tick was gorging itself, but no matter how many times she scratched or rubbed, the pain persisted.

Tia frowned. A lock above her right ear had worked its way free of the pins securing it in place. Drat.

A knock at the door interrupted her inspection. Steward Bennett's inquiry came through the door, asking if she was ready.

"One moment!" Tia jammed the errant strands of hair back in place, pricking her fingers in three places. Wincing, she eyed the digits. Sure enough, tiny red dots marred her skin. Just wonderful.

Bennett's voice penetrated the door. "The master awaits."

Tia let out an exasperated sigh and wiped away the bloodstains. "I'm coming." More aches and pains passed through her body as she walked across the room. The thick cloth pressed into her shoulders. She could barely breathe. And her right shoe kept catching on the hem.

She reached the door, threw it open. Bennett stood there, prim, and proper, dressed in a faded blue suit with gold buttons. A smile creased his lips. "This way, my lady."

He took Tia's hand and guided her along a dim corridor lined with dark shapes. Tia pursed her lips. Shadows filled the corridor.

They reached the entry to Ian's study. Strange.

Bennett opened the portal and stood aside. A single weak light gleamed from within, illuminating the Baron's desk and little else. "The master wishes to discuss certain matters before the ceremony."

Tia's mind whirled. Yes, there were a million details to be settled regarding the betrothal and attached commercial contracts. But the important items were settled – weren't they?

Bennett urged her into the chamber.

"Ian, darling?" *Tia could see the Baron's overstuffed chair, but its occupant was lost in shadow.* "What's so important it couldn't wait?" *Probably it had to do with Peter being named overlord of Groveton. The insufferable idiot was utterly unsuited for the post.*

"Where's the priestess?" *Ian's voice came from with the chair's depths, but the Baron himself was almost invisible.*

"Priestess?" *Tia was baffled.* "I don't understand. Father Barnabas is performing the service." *She'd wished a higher-ranking cleric to officiate, but none were available. Was that what Ian was asking about?*

"Father Barnabas's superior," *said Ian.* "She arranged all this."

"Ian, what are you talking about?" *Was he drunk? His speech didn't sound slurred, but that meant nothing.*

"I'm talking about the priestess who lured you into Cosslet. It wasn't even on your original itinerary."

"Ian!" *Tia couldn't keep the shock from her voice.* "That was Peter's doing. You know that. Besides, what does it matter?"

"Oh, it matters." *Ian rose from his chair and stepped into the light.*

Tia gasped and stepped back. Ian looked horrible – no, monstrous. His face was hard planes and cruel angles. His eyes gleamed red. A severe black and gray suit encased his body. "Ian, what's wrong? You're scaring me."

"Wrong?" *Ian cocked his head.* "Well, you for one." *He took a step towards Tia.*

Tia took another step back. Her body connected with the wall. "Ian, why"-

The Baron's hand lashed out, quick as a striking snake. Fingers with the strength of steel gripped her throat. "Your presence here is no accident. He noticed you." Ian's head filled Tia's vision. Dark shapes moved in his red eyes. "Have you any idea how rare that is? I had him convinced, committed. Now he doubts. Just a little, but enough to inconvenience me."

Tia tried to speak, but only a strangled squawk escaped her throat. Her vision blurred.

Ian released his grip.

Tia slid to the floor in a heap.

"I should kill you here and now." Ian stared into space and talked to himself. "He will be upset. However, your presence makes him less pliable."

Tia slid towards the entry.

A booted foot blocked her path. A massive weight slammed into Tia's chest. She couldn't breathe. A black void filled her vision.

Ian's voice reached her from a great distance. "No. You are not slithering away from me. Your subversions require payment in pain."

Tia attempted to follow the lunatic logic. "Won't," she gasped, "that just," gasp, "make him mad?"

Ian's hand filled Tia's vision. Sharp agony exploded against her right cheek. "Don't presume to dictate to me!"

"How" – Tia choked the word out, "very," gasp, "brave of you."

The boot paused. "Bravery means nothing. I do what is necessary." Ian's voice sounded different.

Realization struck Tia like a thunderclap. "You are not Ian."

The angular face contorted into a cruel grin. "Oh, but I am Ian - the husband of your fears. And now that fear will destroy you."

The boot descended.

Tia braced herself, knowing pain and death awaited. She closed her eyes.

The expected impact didn't come. Tia opened her eyelids.

Ian towered over her with his face twisted into a new expression – bafflement. "How? What?" Then he vanished.

TIA AWOKE FROM NIGHTMARE into dire reality. She stared at an angled ceiling lit by orange lanterns. A tent. Strange, discordant music seeped through walls, unlike any Tia had heard, even in Solaces decadent nightspots. Hard pain bit into her wrists and ankles when she tried to sit. She craned her head sideways, spotted a man in quality attire atop a rude cot, bound hand, and foot.

Tia blinked "Ian?"

Ian stared at her. "Tia?"

"So, you're awake, cousin." Charles appeared between the pair. "This will be so much more satisfying."

"Charles?" Ian blinked. "What are you doing?"

"Claiming what is mine by right." Charles motioned at a pair of swarthy men wearing multicolored clothes. Gypsies. "Take him."

"Don't," said Tia.

Charles whirled and bent over her. "My, my, everybody is awake."

A feminine shriek of pain and fear overrode the music. Charles cocked his head. "That was Vanessa." He glared at Ian. "You're next."

Vanessa. Dead. Tia couldn't wrap her mind around the thought.

"Murdering your way to my seat?" Ian tried to rise, failed. "Is that what this madness is?"

"Oh, it's more than that, cousin. Much more." He snapped his fingers. The gypsies grasped Ian by the head and ankles. Ian struggled to no avail. "Pity you won't be here to see it."

The gypsies carried Ian from the tent.

Charles started after them, paused, and turned to Tia. "You'll be joining him shortly."

Images from the nightmare seeped into this insane reality. "Won't killing me make him mad?"

Charles froze. "You know too much. But not enough." He exited the tent in a jerky walk, not his normal fluid movement.

"I wanna go home."

Tia recognized the voice. Celina. She flipped her head and spied the child trussed up on another cot. Past her, another shape wiggled and flopped on the floor. "I want to go home too."

A red-stained length of steel poked through the tent flap, followed by Peter. Behind him, Kyle's bulk filled the entryway. Like the Knight, he carried a blood-smeared sword.

"Tia! I thought that was your voice." Peter rushed to her side.

"Peter!" Relief flooded Tia. "It's Charles. He's going to kill Ian."

"Charles. That explains a couple matters." He stepped close to Tia. "Hold out your arms." A bronze knife appeared in his free hand.

"Me, too uncle." Celina managed to wiggle herself into a sitting position. "Garrets almost free."

The knife cut through two of the strands binding Tia's wrists. "How many are in here?" asked Peter.

Celina counted on her fingers. "There's me and Tia and Garret and Rodney and Sarah and two more I don't know. Eight."

"Too many." Peter's quiet words carried across the confined space.

"My hands are free," said Tia. "Give me a knife."

Peter produced a dagger from his belt and handed it to her hilt first. "Cut Celina free while I get these cords off your legs."

"There! Got it." Garret slipped free of his bonds.

Peter glanced at the flap. "Kyle, give the kid a knife."

The big man took a single giant step inside the tent and gave the youth a dagger. He cast a worried look in Peter's direction. "We must hurry. Something is coming."

Tia freed Celina at the same time Peter hacked the cords binding her feet. Garret sawed industriously at the ropes binding a young woman.

Kyle returned to the entry. "This is taking too long."

"We're going as fast as we can." Tia shot Kyle a black look. Why didn't he free them with his magic? She shook her head. What was she thinking? This was Kyle. Tia stepped to a prostrate man on the floor. She ran the knife over the ropes binding his wrists.

Beside her, Peter severed the bonds of a boy.

"It's here." The creaks and groans of shattering wood accompanied Kyle's words.

Tia's limbs froze from sheer terror. 'What's here,' she wanted to ask. But her mouth refused to work, and she feared the answer.

"We're out of time." Peter cut a slit through the back wall. He grabbed Tia's arm and thrust her at the opening. "Run! Keep silent."

Behind him, Kyle chanted arcane words amidst a cascade of blue and white sparks that cast an eerie light into the tent.

Tia stumbled through the slit and into a tangle of dark shrubbery that grasped at her dress. Twigs and branches grabbed at her as she pushed into the darkness. Other figures thrashed beside her, accompanied by panicked voices.

But that paled to the ungodly cacophony behind her.

EMPIRE: COUNTRY IXX – Peter

Creaks, pops, and thuds penetrated the canvas as something big smashed through the wagon outside the tent.

Other men, unused to combating infernal foes, would have been paralyzed with fear. But Peter and Kyle were veterans of the Traag War, where demons roamed the battlefields.

"We're out of time." Peter grabbed Tia's arm with one hand and made a long vertical slit in the tent wall with the other.

Behind them, arcane words gushed from Kyle's mouth.

Peter tried to propel Tia towards the gap, but she remained rooted to the spot, eyes wide, body trembling. "Run!" He spoke the word directly into her ear. "Keep silent."

The knight's words penetrated Tia's terror. Tia stumbled through the gap, closely followed by Celina, Garret, and another woman.

Peter spun to face the main entry, sword in one hand, brass dagger in the other.

Kyle's incantation ended in a choked gasp and the sound of a heavy object slamming into the bushes.

Then the whole tent was torn away, and Peter stood in a square patch of dirt staring at an abomination. It resembled a droath: big, six-legged, but with far too many tentacles. Its flesh seemed partially transparent, lit from within by yellow and red spheres. A god-awful stench reached his nostrils, worse than an open sewer or garbage pit. H knew that smell from the war. Demon.

Common steel didn't bite demons – only church magic and blessed blades. Peter wielded the later against the abominations a dozen times during the war. Thrice, he'd even given death blows to such creatures if such could truly perish. But today he possessed no such weapon.

A calm certainty swept over Peter. Today he would die. He accepted that. But just maybe he could buy Tia and Celina the opportunity to escape.

My sword and talisman are one. Something pricked Peter's chest.

"Are you ready to die, little pest?" The horrid blubbering voice came from the droath-demon.

"Are you, creature of the pit?" Peter made an elaborate twisting swing with the sword. The blade solidly connected with a tentacle thicker than his thigh and longer than he was tall, but instead of severing or even scratching the appendage, there was merely a sizzling sound, accompanied by blue-white sparks.

"Little fool," bellowed the blubbering demon, "Iron cannot bite me."

Peter feinted left, then ducked right as a tree-truck tentacle flashed over his head.

Kyle's voice sounded in the darkness, working another incantation.

Colored sparks flashed along the droath-demon's hide. "Pathetic fool. Your pitiful spells cannot touch me." Its tentacles uprooted a stand of small trees.

Again, Peter felt that pinprick at his breast. *You bear my talisman. Now take my blade. They go together, one into the other.* And then he knew. He reached beneath his shirt and yanked the Mithraic amulet from his chest. It slid right into the wooden handle of the bronze knife.

He rolled to his feet and charged the fell creature, it's bulk looming over him. His sword slammed into the things side. Again, it bounced off amidst a cascade of colored sparks.

The droath-demon rose on its hind appendages, exposing a tentacle lined maw large enough to swallow a cow.

Peter tensed. Steel wasn't going to win this battle. One chance. Time to do the one thing no swordsman ever did. The knight's sword came up – and went airborne as the weapon left his hand.

A lashing tentacle deflected the blade. "See, fool, there is nothing you can do to hurt me," blubbered that obscene voice. An obscenely flexible limb swatted at Peter.

But Peter wasn't there. Instead, mind utterly focused, he threw himself right at the creature, the now-glowing knife held before him. Sparks flashed along the blade – and then the knife was buried in the demon's guts, straining for the glowing shapes in its innards.

"Aiieeaaahooo!" The monstrosity recoiled. "This cannot be!"

Peter ducked a thrashing tentacle, dug in his heels, and threw his full weight at the creature. His hand and forearm sunk into its slimy, putrid hide. The blades tip pierced the first glowing organ, extinguishing it.

"Ahooiieee!" The droath-demon bucked, lifting the knight from the ground.

Peter ignored his pain and pressed the blade deeper into the infernal. Gruesome flesh coated his biceps. The glowing knife pierced another luminous mass.

The droath-demon collapsed into a gelatinous mass. "Iron cannot bite..."

Peter rolled away from the bulk. "The knife was bronze, not iron."

"You killed my Shoggoth," Silam's voice cut through the night. "Have you any notion how difficult it was to conjure her? I had to sacrifice an entire village."

Thrashing noises came from the undergrowth. Hopefully, that was the prisoners making their escape. He should go after them. Tia needed protection. He took a step towards the bushes.

Peter stopped. Ian. Tia said Charles intended to kill Ian.

He scanned the area. Lights suspended from poles illuminated a path climbing a gradual rise where barely discernable figures intoning a monosyllabic chant gathered around a stone table. No, not a table, an altar.

Two figures jerked a third to his feet. Despite the distance, Peter recognized Ian immediately. He broke into a run.

Thirty paces out. The trail broke into a clearing. Pools of light shined on twisted, disemboweled bodies. Peter recognized some of them. John Cell. Jason Rodriguez. The innkeeper.

Twenty paces from the altar. The two men bent Ian over the stone slab. The Baron wiggled and flopped to no avail. Behind him, a short stump of a woman in the black and red robes of an agban sorceress raised a wicked knife, screaming an incantation not meant for human lips. Peter recognized her: Mother Shrub, an herb witch who'd appeared in Cosslet after the war. He put on a burst of speed.

Ten paces out. Peter put on a burst of speed. He might just make it – then a heavy weight slammed into him from the side. Peter fell to the ground in a tangle of limbs and searing pain.

"I can't let you stop it." Charles's eyes were wide above a lunatic grin. A sword dangled loosely from one hand. "It's my time. He promised."

Peter's side burned as he leaped to his feet. "Fool." He charged the Forester, sword positioned for a killing stroke.

Charles leaped aside, landed atop a corpse, and fell into darkness.

Peter whirled. His cousin was invisible. Worse, he was better suited to fighting in the dark. The cursed music masked any sound he might make. A horrible scream came from the hillock. Peter turned his head as in Ian's lifeless body rolled from the altar. Mother Shrub stood behind the slab, knife still raised, chanting.

"He's dead," Peter spoke the words aloud without realizing it. Ian was dead. The energy drained from his limbs. He'd failed to rescue Ian. Just like he'd failed Tessa.

Every joint in his body ached. Just standing took tremendous effort. His side stung.

Movement caught his eye. Charles? No, too big. Kyle. Peter took a breath. He strode towards the big man. Tessa was dead. Ian was dead. But Tia still needed protection. And Silam needed killing.

EMPIRE: COUNTRY XX – Kyle

Magic filled the air – literally. Mystic lines and clouds of arcane power permeated Kyles Sight, almost overriding his normal vision. But it was tainted. Blood magic. Hundreds of lives had been ritually extinguished to raise this power.

And those responsible knew of Kyle's presence. They knew he'd overcome the ward demon and escaped. Now, an entity that Kyle perceived as an arcane nexus approached the tent where he stood guard. He'd warned Peter that danger approached, but the fool knight didn't listen. Typical highborn.

Power flared and a wagon exploded into splinters. "It's here!"

Kyle recited his meager protective charm. A tree-trunk thick appendage slammed into the massive magician. Air escaped his lungs in a giant 'whoosh' as magical sparks played across his body. He felt his feet leave the ground. A branch cracked across his back and side with burning force. Twigs whipped into the big man's limbs and stung his face. He crashed into a tangled mass of shrubbery.

Hot pain erupted in Kyle's ribs when he tried to draw a breath. Darkness closed in at the edge of his Sight. He inhaled again, ignoring the agony. Cool night air reached his lungs. The pain receded a fraction. Then he stood.

The tent was gone, replaced by the demon, a house-sized abomination comprised of tentacles and roles of putrid, semi-transparent flesh, illuminated from within by glowing nodes – the source of the creature's power, the energy that permitted it to exist in the mortal realm. Serpentine limbs lashed at a tiny figure confronting it: Sir Peter, wielding his captured sword in one hand and that bronze knife in the other.

Mortals who battled demons with normal steel died. Entities akin to this one slaughtered entire legion's during the war.

Kyle hesitated. He should leave. With his magic, he might win free of this place, and then – what? Add yet another nightmare to the ones he already carried? No. He focused his mind and summoned fire, willing the demons flesh to ignite.

Sparks played across the demon's hide where his magic connected, but the spell didn't take root. *Warded. I should have spotted that.*

A tentacle lashed at Kyle. The big man hurled himself beneath a mat of interlocking branches as the appendage struck with the force of an avalanche. The shrubbery absorbed the blow - but now he was trapped.

Frantic, half crushed by the weight from above, Kyle attempted to escape by wiggling still deeper into the briar patch.

The tentacle whipped away, and a horrific, inhuman cry of pain and outrage filled the night as the demon died. Unbelievable. Somehow, the fool knight had accomplished the impossible. That bronze knife. It had to be blessed somehow.

"You killed my Shoggoth." Kyle recognized Silam's voice. Connections formed in the mages mind as he fought his way through the thicket. Droath. Shoggoth. The same. His detection spell had worked. The realization brought grim satisfaction. No time for recriminations. Kyle grunted and forced a path through the brush.

The vegetation thinned enough to where he could stand.

A godawful shriek, louder than the chaotic music, turned his head. Ahead and above, his Sight revealed a nexus of power fed by terror and bound by blood and stone. Arcane lines invisible to mortal perception funneled that energy to a warded point left of his position. That was where Silam would be. Protective spells guarded the Saban. But the altar – that was vulnerable.

Lanterns suspended from posts made a path to the altar. Good enough.

Kyle strode towards the lights, tripped, slipped, and landed on something soft, wet, and sticky. He blinked, used a minor cantrip to adjust his perception. Blood covered his hands. His gut churned.

Kyle rose on trembling legs. He stood in a field of butchered bodies, chests ripped open, their mouths wide in terror. There. That was Bennet, the Baron's steward, staring blindly at the night sky, one arm draped over Marta's plump corpse. Simon's dead eyes gazed at him from atop a mound of corpses. And that body there – no. Kyle fell to his knees, sobbing, staring at Amelia's lifeless features.

"She's gone," said Peter's voice from beside him.

Kyle didn't turn. The sobs wouldn't stop.

A hand slammed into his face. Peter's voice cut through the night. "She's dead. So is my brother. They're beyond saving. But we can still kill Silam."

Kyle faced the knight. Peter's face was scarred mask. He carried a knife that gleamed in Kyle's Sight. "I can't."

Peters hand connected with his face a second time. "Enough whining. Buck up, legionary."

Pain penetrated sorrow. Kyle rose to his feet and glared at the knight. He raised his fist.

The knight stood his ground. "Direct your ire at those responsible for this carnage."

A ragged sob escaped Kyle. Confronting Silam was suicide, but with Amelia dead, what did he have to live for? Answer: vengeance. "Ok."

Peter relaxed a fraction. A tight smile creased his face. "Good. Now, let's find Silam and Charles."

Kyle shook his head. "I know where Silam is – but my magic can't touch him. Your knife might."

"Fine, then. Lead the way."

Kyle scanned the area with senses both normal and supernatural. Possibilities emerged. There. And there.

"Follow." He lumbered to the lantern path and uprooted a post, a wooden shaft with the length and heft of a spear. Liquid sloshed when he shook the lamp. Good. At least a third full. It always amazed him the how much energy was locked away in oil. Fumar branches would have been better, but oil would work.

Post in one hand, lantern in the other, he reversed course.

Peter placed a hand on his shoulder. "What are you doing?"

Kyle cringed at another horrible scream of terror. "Ending this," he said as the cry faded. "Ending all of it." He shook off Peter's hand.

They reached a point midway between the altar and a cluster of lights marking Silam's position. Any closer, and the Saban sorcerer would know their location - if he didn't already. He gripped the lantern and focused his mind on the oil reservoir, on all the energy locked within that dark liquid. Then he threw the lamp as hard as he could.

Silam's voice cut through the night. "Kyle, do you really expect such a pathetic effort to breach my wards?"

Peter shared a similar sentiment as the lamp arced off into the darkness. "What'd you do that for? It's nowhere near him." He motioned at the lights.

"Stay close." Kyle focused his will on the descending light. "Be ready." He wrapped a massive arm around the knight's waist.

The lantern struck the trunk of a giant cottonwood that leaned over the clearing. Now. A thunderous blast and a gout of flame engulfed entire tree.

"Kyle, your aim is beyond pathetic." Silam sounded amused.

Creaks and pops sounded from the trunk. The cottonwood tilted. Transformed into a gigantic, prickly torch that shed flaming fragments of itself as ever louder creaks and pops erupted from its base. The flaming bole leaned over the clearing, seemed to hover over the infernal altar.

A shrill voice from that bloodstained stone began a frantic incantation. Too little, too late. With a final massive pop, the fiery knot of branches atop the trunk slammed directly atop the altar, splitting the stone in twain amidst a flurry of screams. The arcane lines connecting the sacrificial platform with Silam vanished.

"Kyle, I stand corrected." Silam sounded upset. "Your aim is annoying."

"Hold tight." Kyle tightened his grip on Peter. He studied the ward spells about the Saban. There. The altars destruction had created a gap.

Kyle invoked a spell he'd performed on three prior occasions. He vanished, taking Peter with him.

EMPIRE: COUNTRY XXI – Tia

Fear propelled Tia through the brush. Unseen branches slapped at her face. Invisible undergrowth pulled at her body. The scratches and pain didn't register. Only escape mattered.

Then she struck an obstacle that refused to budge. Something harder than wood. Stone. A boulder?

Tia stretched her hands to either side, probing, searching for a route past the barrier. Her fingers found crevices the rock joined others. A wall. Tia sobbed. Who would build a wall out here? She twisted sideways, found a gap through the shrubbery, and slithered past the obstruction.

Knee-high weeds replaced the brush.

Light drew her attention to a bonfire atop a low knoll, next to a stone platform. The ugly little witch 'Mother Shrub' stood on the far side of this slab, clad in a robe of red and black, a wavy bladed dagger in one hand.

A pair of gypsies dragged a bound figure with curly hair towards the altar – for that was what that flat slab was, sure as anything – and heaved their burden down atop it.

Tia glimpsed the doomed man's face. Ian! Tia's covered her mouth as the knife plummeted into the Baron's guts.

Tia ran. Her foot slipped on something firm yet soft and slick. She toppled onto a sticky; pliant mass surrounded by a sewer stench.

Tia raised her head. Blinked. And suppressed another scream.

Vanessa's sightless eyes stared back at her. A gaping hole rimmed in blood marred the center of the dead girl's chest. A youth's head projected from beneath Vanessa's body. Bitter bile rose in Tia's throat.

Tia stood on shaky legs. Her head rotated. More bodies appeared in the predawn gloom. Stewards Bennet and Kessler shared an obscene bed of cadavers. Consul Sigrid's corpse sat propped against a brown shape – no, that was Father Barnabas. Masters Anatoly and Nikolas crowned a hillock of corpses. Dead men, women, and children surrounded her. Dozens of them. No, scores. Maybe hundreds. *Everybody who attended the performance. Everybody but me.*

Tia screamed and ran from the carnage. She needed to hide. She ducked past a tilted tree. Was that a gap? An exit? Heart pounding, Tia pushed through the underbrush and into an open area.

An ebony figure detached itself from the darkness. Silam.

The wizard gazed at her. "Ah, Lady Samos." The light glinted off his teeth as he smiled. "How considerate of you to join me."

Tia tried to retreat. Her feet refused to move. The horrid music seemed louder than ever.

Silam shook his head and wagged a finger at her. "Now, now, Lady Samos. You can't leave. We must speak." He paused. "And then you need to die."

Tia found her voice. "Murderer! You killed them all, curse you."

"Now, now, whatever happened to your manners?" Silam's tone held the mildest of rebukes. "You can't hope to impress a noble swain with such course speech. Not that it matters at this point."

"You murdered them. Ian – Bennet – Vanessa – all the others"-

Silam lifted a hand and Tia felt her mouth clamp shut. "No, Mother Shrub killed those people. She's an Agban sorceress, you know, perhaps the last one east of the Shadow Sea."

The Saban cocked his head. "Kyle, do you really expect such a pathetic effort to breach my wards?"

What was Silam talking about? Was Kyle out there? Was he trying to fight back?

A flying light struck the massive tree behind Tia. A thunderous roar filled Tia's ears. Blazing twigs and bits of bark rained upon her.

Silam was unfazed by the blast. "Kyle," he said in a tone of dark amusement, "your aim is pathetic."

Tia agreed with the sorcerer. Kyle's throw didn't come anywhere near the Saban.

An immense 'pop' almost drowned out Silam's last word. More pops followed, along with a series of creaks and deep groans. The tree tilted more. Then it kept right on falling – straight onto the hilltop altar, which split in twain with a loud 'crack' and chorus of screams.

"I stand corrected." Silam stared at the wreck with an impassive expression, though his voice betrayed irritation. "Your aim is annoying."

The Saban wizard reeled backward as a large shape in a tattered blue coat slammed into him. Behind him, another man in filthy evening attire stumbled into view, clenching his head.

Tia blinked.

Kyle's arms caged Silam's torso and left arm. He heaved the Saban into the air.

Hope ignited in Tia's breast.

Peter charged Silam with a raised shortsword in one hand and a bronze knife in the other.

The Saban's free hand grabbed the weapon's hilt.

Undeterred, Peter stabbed Silam with the knife.

Silam twisted as the blade struck his torso. A groan escaped the Saban. "That hurt." His gaze focused on the knife. "You have it? But how?"

Tia's body tingled.

Peter struck again, cutting Silam's forearm.

Silam grabbed Peter's chest. "Enough." Impossibly, he broke Kyles's grip, twisted, and grabbed the big man's coat front. Then he pushed. Both men flew backward into the darkness.

Tia shrieked, turned, and ran, blind with terror. Three steps later she slammed full tilt into something soft and flexible and went down in a tumbled heap.

The music stopped. Tia stared into the eyes of a Chou man in a green robe pulling himself to a sitting position. Rebecca sprawled on the ground behind him.

The Chou man stood, still staring at her. "You came," he said in his native language, "but do you know me?"

Tia stared at him, uncomprehending. What madness was this? Of course, she didn't know him. She didn't know him at all, outside of that strange dream. Dreams. An impossible thought occurred to her. "Li-Pang?"

"Ah, you do know me." The flautists head bobbed. "Good, good."

"Not good," said Silam in the chou language. "She's a pointless, useless distraction, nothing more."

Li-Pang stood. His eyes flicked to Silam. "She is more than that."

"Hah!" Silam spat.

Li-Pang stared at the demolished altar. "You sought to blind me to yet another atrocity, I see."

"It was necessary." Silam sounded deferential.

Tia sat with her eyes wide open. She wanted to flee but her feet refused to move.

Li-Pang faced Silam. His features hardened. "I should rid myself of you."

"You cannot. We are one." Silam's voice conveyed weary patience. "You are the shaper, and I am the shaper's shadow. We cannot be separated. You cannot defy yourself."

"I did, though," said the flautist. "Remember?"

Glowing motes in assorted colors drifted through the vegetation.

"You broke the power of the world in twain, wrecked pandemonium, and still failed to sever our bond!"

"You are me, and I am you." Li-Pang sounded like a judge passing an edict. "Therefore, I command myself to leave these people be."

Silam's shoulders slumped. "They killed my Shoggoth."

"Your pet was more trouble than it was worth. It couldn't even distinguish between a priestess and a peasant." Li-Pang brushed away a blue orb.

Silam kicked a root. "They ruined the ritual."

" An unnecessary, pointless, bloody, and certain to attract attention ritual. As always, you undermine yourself."

"Fine." Silam's hands flopped to his side. "She lives. They live. The rite is completed anyhow." He glared at Li-Pang. "But we leave."

Li-Pang's fingers brushed against Tia's face.

A fluorescent pink sphere filled Tia's vision. Her world dissolved.

EMPIRE: COUNTRY XXII – Peter

P eter drifted in a realm of red pain and half-heard voices. Hard dull aches pushed into his right arm and leg. His chest felt heavy. And a sharp pointy object kept digging into his back, right beneath the shoulder blade, making him squirm.

He shifted again, but the pain in his back intensified. A high-pitched sound reached his ears. His eyes flicked open.

Twigs materialized before Peter's face. Past them, weak dawn light illuminated an expanse of trampled brush and grass. He was on his side, atop a curved surface burnt black in places. The tree. He was atop the tree felled by Kyle's spell.

Chaotic memories flooded his brain. The nightmare. The massacre in Drakkar. The old knight - real or imaginary? He remembered stabbing the demon. The altar. Ian, dead. Silam. He struggled to a seated position and clenched his head. What happened?

A scream interrupted his thoughts. "Get away from me!"

Peter recognized the voice. Celina. He dropped to the ground. The aches in his legs multiplied as he struck.

"Come back here, bitch!" A male voice, heavily accented.

Peter strode towards the commotion. Celina shot under his nose. Chasing her was a squat, muscular, dark-skinned man in colorful clothing, carrying a bloodied short sword – one of Silam's gypsies.

The gypsy halted. "You!" The gypsy brandished the weapon. "You kilt Renaldo and Hiram! Murderer!"

Peter acted on reflex. He sidestepped the attacker, grabbed the man's wrists, spun him around and kicked him hard in the gut. The gypsies back slammed into the fallen tree. A sharp gore covered branch erupted from his chest. Blood poured from the gypsy's mouth.

Peter hefted the sword.

"Wow!" Celina materialized, covered in dirt, leaves, and twigs. "You killed him good, uncle."

Peter managed a weak smile. "Anything for my favorite niece."

"We gotta be careful." Celina made a sweeping motion with one hand. "There's more of them out there. That stink-butt Charles is giving them orders."

"Charles? What about Silam?" The magician was the truly dangerous one.

Celina scrunched her face. "I dunno."

Damn. Had Silam abandoned his followers? Would he return? "Did anybody else escape?" Peter leaned against the tree.

"I was with Garret when he found me." Celina motioned at the body. "He ran. They killed Sarah. Rodney's still out there, I think."

"What about Tia? Kyle?"

Celina pointed at a blue lump partially hidden by a bush. "Isn't that Kyle?"

Peter approached the form. Sure enough, it was Kyle.

"Is he dead?"

"Not unless the dead snore." Peter kicked the big man's side.

A 'woof' escaped the oaf's mouth. His eyes opened.

Peter leaned over him. "On your feet, soldier. That's enough sack time."

Kyle groaned and shifted position.

"I found Tia and another lady." Celina's voice came from the side. "They're asleep."

Tia! She's alive! Peter plowed through the underbrush. He burst into a small clearing. Tia and Rebecca lay on a bed of grass, their heads propped against a moss-covered log.

"I tell you, at least two of them ran this way."

"Screw them," said a second voice. "I say we take the horses and leave."

"No, we leave any of them alive, then the Eye's will know who we are," said the first speaker, referring to the common name for Imperial Intelligence. "They'll track us to the empires edge and beyond, if need be."

Two men emerged from the foliage. One was slender, swarthy, and clad in bright colors – another of Silam's gypsies. Brown fur and dark leather marked the second as a woodsman. Both carried bared blades that gleamed red in the morning light.

Both men stopped in their tracks. "It's him," said the fur-clad man. "The knight. The one that kilt the master's pet demon."

"I did." Peter took a step towards the men.

The gypsy pointed at the impaled man. "He kilt Rodrigo!"

"And I'm about to kill you." Peter took another step.

"Hah!" The woodsman spat. "You kin hardly stand, let alone swing that sticker."

A loud groan came from the shrubbery, accompanied by the sound of cracking branches. Kyle lumbered into view, holding a giant tree branch. "Die!" He ran at the men.

Kyle swung before the men could act. Jagged branches on the improvised club impaled the gypsy's chest.

The woodsman attempted to stab the big man.

Kyle released the club as the blade grazed his chest.

Then Peter's sword pierced the rogue's back, adding a crimson stain to the furs.

Kyle looked at Peter, face contorted in anger and sorrow. "Go away! They killed her!" He plopped onto a stump. A tormented wail came from his throat. Tears poured from his eyes.

"He's sad about Amelia." Celina pointed at the field of corpses. "They were going to get married."

Motion past the altar attracted Peter's attention. Horses. A whole herd, forty or more, no doubt used to pull the wagons that brought them to this hellhole. Tia's carriage sat atop a knoll just past the animals, next to a cluster of wagons.

Peter considered Kyle. The big man was volatile, uninclined to go anywhere. He knelt beside Celina. "Stay here with Kyle while I get a carriage hitched."

Celina glanced at the big man, then back at Peter. "Kay."

Peter strode into the meadow. Each step took him past the body of an old friend, acquaintance, or rival. Insects climbed over John Cell's body. Jason Vasquez and his brothers were sprawled in a heap. Steward Bennett and Marta were intertwined in death. Carter. Rodriguez. A crow perched atop Vanessa's head, picking at her eyes. A cloud of bugs swarmed above Trevor the innkeeper and his serving girls.

Peter neared the altar. The corpses became thicker, forming piles that rose past his knees. Crows stood atop these heaps, orbited by dense clouds of bugs.

There. Ian, staring sightlessly at the steel-gray sky, just feet from the altar. Ian, the responsible one who'd paid attention to his studies. Ian, who'd informally banished Peter from Cosslet even as he worked to legitimize his birth. Now, nothing but carrion food.

"Somebody there?" The voice was a cracked whisper.

Peter gripped his sword hilt and strode towards the altar. Three bound men laid alongside the slab. One was dead, pierced through the gut by a branch from the fallen tree. The other two regarded him with wide eyes. Peter recognized none of them. But they were clearly victims.

Peter cut their bonds.

The stouter sat with an effort and rubbed his wrists. "Sir Peter?"

Peter nodded.

"I'm Frederick." He stretched. "I work for Trevor, in the stables."

Peter motioned at the slope. "Your boss is down there with the rest."

Frederick winced. He averted his gaze from the corpses.

"There are other survivors near the trees." Peter sliced through Frederick's bonds. "I could use some help hitching up a carriage to take us from this place."

"Suits me." Frederick stood and nudged the other man in the ribs with his boot. "Come on Bert."

Peter took a step from the broken slab. A raspy sound from the tree's far side made him pause. Had somebody else survived? He negotiated a path through the thicket of branches.

There: a wrinkled white face tucked within ragged black and red fabric. Mother Shrub, skewered by a dozen branches, yet still clinging to life.

Her eyes flicked open. "You killed my mate when we came here to erect Kato-Siva's altar."

Peter blinked. He recalled stabbing a bald man clad in a black and red robe in a forest clearing. He'd been a kid of fifteen. "I remember."

"Good." The woman's head moved a fraction. "Now I have killed all you hold dear and offered their essence to the Great Ones."

"Kato-Siva is dead." Peter rammed his sword through the witches' eye. "And now, so are you." He pulled the sword free and strode over to rejoin Frederic.

Buttons and Ginger cropped grass next to Peter's steed and two others. Tack dangled from Ginger's flanks.

Peter inspected his horse. The gelding didn't have a scratch. He shook his head.

Bert ambled over as Peter checked the saddlebags. "I recollect this place. Fort Cragmoor."

Peter nodded. Cragmoor was an old legion encampment inside the Kirkwood. It'd changed hands at least thrice during the Occupation. "I thought it was flooded out."

"The west half, yes." Bert pointed at a lengthy line of hitched together wagons. "That track leads to the old East Gate." He moved his arm to the other track, the one with Tia's carriage. "This one goes through the north side. The roads should hook together."

Peter nodded. Legion encampments always boasted a gate in each cardinal direction. "I'll get the others."

Bert and Frederick hitched the horses to Tia's carriage.

Peter found Kyle and Celina beside each other on a log, talking. Or rather, Celina was doing the talking while Kyle tossed in a grunt now and again. Tia and Rebecca were still asleep on their mossy bed.

Celina hopped up at Peter's approach. "I found something for you, uncle." She held out the bronze knife. "I remember you had this."

"Thank you." Peter felt a faint tingle when his fingers touched the hilt. Or maybe it was a spasm. He tucked the knife in his belt and strode over to the women. "Kyle, give me a hand."

The big man glared at him but didn't rise.

"Do you want to remain here, surrounded by corpses?" Peter waved at the meadow.

Kyle grunted and stood. Twigs and dirt fell from his body. Then he lumbered over to the women, knelt, and threw Rebecca over his shoulder like a sack of potatoes. "You get Tia." He turned and strode towards the carriage without waiting for a response.

Peter knelt and shook Tia. No response. He hooked his arms under her neck and knees and stood. She weighed much less than he expected. Then he set out after Kyle, trailed by Celina.

"Garret!" Celina darted ahead of Peter as they neared the carriage, making a beeline straight for a slender youth.

Bert stepped from behind a wagon as they approached. He carried a jug in one hand and had a sack slung over his shoulder. "Found some victuals."

"That's good work." Peter's stomach rumbled.

Kyle glared at Frederick, still perched in the carriages driver's seat. "That's my spot."

"Let's leave this place," said Peter.

EMPIRE: COUNTRY XXIII - Tia

*T*ia *walked across a field of bright flowers dotted with immense black boulders. Deformed black-haired men with ochre skin perched atop these monoliths, leering at Tia as they banged on drums strapped to their chests.*

A huge wolf-like creature stepped from behind a plinth and regarded Tia with yellow eyes.

Tia froze.

The monster charged.

Tia turned and ran as the tempo increased, frantically seeking refuge from the beast, but there was nothing save pretty flowers and sheer-sided obelisks.

Then a weight pushed at Tia's side, forcing her to the ground. She felt the beast's hot breath upon her neck.

"NO!" THE FLOWER FIELD melted into a wooden wall as Tia awoke. But the drumming sound remained as did the weight pressing into her side.

Tia craned her neck. Rebecca, sound asleep, leaned against her. A filthy Celina sat past the gypsy, staring into space while weaving her fingers together.

Tia pushed Rebecca to an upright position and took in the figures on the opposite bench: three men, two older and one younger, each clad in simple tunics. The youth appeared familiar – one of Celina's friends?

The carriage lurched, and Tia's head smacked into the wall. She grimaced and straightened herself. "What happened? I remember Silam and"- she stopped speaking as images of pale corpses appeared in her head.

The stoutest man shifted position. His right hand rested on the hilt of an unsheathed short sword. "The sorcerer abandoned his minions." His brow furrowed. "That place was Fort Cragmoor – an old legion encampment with an evil reputation. A most unwise location to spend Doom Day."

"God above!" Tia's pulse quickened. She'd forgotten about that horrific holiday. "Thank you for enlightening me, Mister–"

"Frederick." He motioned at the scrawny fellow next to him. "Bert. That's Garret against the wall."

"My father's name is Frederick." It sounded inane, but nothing else came to Tia's mind.

Banging and scraping sounds came through the wagon's walls. Tia started. It sounded as though savage beasts sought entry to finish the cultists slaughter.

Frederick made a halfhearted calming motion. "Just twigs and branches striking the sides, my lady. The road is overgrown. But we will win through. We must. The Forest Road is nearby."

The coach stopped. Tia made to open the door.

Frederick placed his hand on her arm. "That would be unwise, my lady. The scoundrels that took us still linger."

"Oh." Tia's heart pounded as she withdrew her hand.

Branches thrashed alongside the carriage. Kyle's maimed face filled the window. He'd acquired two new scars, both leaking blood.

"Deadfall ahead."

"Ok." Frederick nudged Bert. "Come on."

Garret rose.

Frederic restrained him. "Best stay here, lad."

"Kyle?"

The Oafs head swiveled. "Stay here." No courtesies. More than a little rage boiled within that big frame. *He lost someone in that massacre. We all did.*

Twigs scraped against the door when Frederick opened it. He dropped to the ground, followed by Bert.

Tia sat and fretted, hands in her lap, as chopping sounds interspersed with curses came from outside the carriage.

"Ok, heave!" Tia recognized Peter's voice. Snapping branches and rustling grass followed the command.

"Argh!"

Tia's heart pounded.

Garret's head snapped towards a window. "They're attacking us."

"I'm hit!" Was that Bert? Tia didn't recognize the voice.

Garret's hand reached for the latch.

"Stay here." Tia's voice cracked as she spoke.

"Where are they?" Frederick.

Something slammed hard into the wagon, almost knocking Tia to the floor. She repressed the urge to scream.

"Got him!" Sir Peter. "Kyle, go that way!"

More thrashing sounds. Then a hard 'crack' next to Tia's head, and a rush of air past her ear. Tia blinked, then stared wide-eyed at the arrow quivering in the opposite wall.

Tia risked a glance through the window and saw Kyle's broad form plowing through the underbrush, sword raised. The big man reached an oddly shaped stump and pivoted. His blade fell. The stump screamed and fell.

The door opened. Frederick fell inside, blood seeping through his sleeve.

"What happened?"

"Ambush." Frederick yanked the arrow from the wall and collapsed next to Garret. "Bert almost took an arrow through the throat."

"What about Charles?" Tia leaned towards him. "Was he there?"

"I don't know." Frederick shook his head. "We killed two. They were women." He stared at the floor.

"They've run." Peter's voice. "The roads clear. We need to leave."

The carriage jolted into motion. Branches raked against the side. The whole conveyance jolted and rocked. Then the noises fell away, save for the 'clomp' of hooves and the rumble of wheels against stones.

"We're on the Kirkwood Road," said Garret.

Frederick glanced out the window. "I pray we reach Cosslet before nightfall."

Tia agreed. Nobody traveled on Hell Day without an excellent reason. Darkness brought with it unholy storms and vengeful ghosts. Sane folk spent this day in a good church with strong wards and sacred music.

"The demons won't get us," said Celina. "Uncle Peter will chop their heads off and Kyle will turn them into mice."

That comment elicited a pained chuckle from Frederick. "Big guy's a sorcerer? He doesn't look it."

Celina glared at him. "He can make fire."

"Oh." Frederick fell back, face pale.

Tia leaned towards him. "Let me see that arm. I studied medicine at the University." She didn't add those studies consisted of just three introductory courses. But doctoring gave her something to do besides fretting and worrying.

"Ok." Frederick pulled back his sleeve, exposing a deep gash. "Damn gypsy got me good."

Tia eyed the injury. "This requires stitches." She felt along the hem of her dress. Miraculously, the needle and thread tucked there for emergency repairs were still in place. "Hold still."

The carriage jolted as Kyle hit a pothole. Tia jabbed Frederick's arm in the wrong spot.

"Ouch!"

Tia withdrew the needle, thought about cursing Kyle, and decided against it. Today was cursed enough without adding to it. "As still as you can, anyhow." She gripped Frederick's arm. "Let's try this again." She pressed the needle into Frederick's flesh and pulled the thread through after it.

The stitches were ragged and uneven. Frederick often jerked as Tia plied the needle. But her efforts closed the wound and staunched the bleeding.

Garret refused to watch. Celina eyed the procedure with fascination. "I want to learn to do that someday."

"Maybe you will." Tia eyed her bloodstained hands. "I need to clean up."

"Here." Celina produced an old shirt. "I found this back there."

The wagon rumbled onward. Conversation seized. Rebecca remained limp as a rag.

Tia worried: Would Charles attack again? What of Silam? Her memories were scant, jumbled.

At length, the carriage turned and stopped. Sir Peter's face appeared outside the window, still astride his steed. "We're at a stream. The horses need water."

Frederick motioned at a sack protruding from beneath Tia's bench. "There's vittles there. Bread, fruit, and meat." He licked his lips. "A splash of wine as well."

They descended from the coach, Garret carrying the sack. Outside, they found Kyle unhitching Buttons and Ginger while Peter led his horse to the river.

The stream was wide, deep, and dark, crossed by a stone bridge covered in moss. Under other conditions, Tia might have found it romantic. Today, though, it looked sinister.

"Sir Peter," called Tia. "We have provisions."

"Good. I'm starved." Peter stumped towards them while his horse drank.

Tia noticed the bronze knife stuck in his belt. "Wherever did you get that?"

Peter bit into an apple and swallowed. "The knife? The blade part was the puppet knights sword. It was in the wagon when I awoke. It... helped me."

Kyle lumbered over to the gathering and grabbed a biscuit.

Tia spotted a metal icon worked into the wooden hilt. "That's Mithras's symbol."

"It is," said Peter. "That is the other part. Father Barnabas gave it to me." He finished the apple and threw the core away.

"Strange they should fit together so." Tia took a bite from a biscuit.

"Can I see that?" asked Kyle around a mouthful of bread.

Peter handed him the knife, hilt first. The big man's eyes lost focus as he rubbed the handle. "Thought so. It's enchanted. Lots of spells folded together."

"For what purpose?" asked Tia.

"I dunno." Kyle shrugged. "Ritual work, maybe. I bet it belonged to a bishop or a cardinal. I wonder..." He slid the symbol from the knifes hilt. His eyes assumed that distant, tranced look. Then he blinked and shrugged his head. "Weird. Neither has any magic when they're apart." He reinserted the token and handed the knife back to Peter.

"How did a country priest obtain such a remarkable relic?" asked Tia.

Peter shrugged. "He said a priestess gave him the symbol. I don't know how the puppet knight came to have the blade."

"That same priestess gave the woodworker the knife. Strange that they should come together so." Tia pursed her lips. "I wonder who this priestess was?"

"Sister Miriam," said Frederick. "She arrived a couple weeks back and settled in at the old monastery."

"Sister Miriam," said Kyle. "I met her at Stone Hollow." The big man's hand went to his chest. He pulled the tattered remnants of his shirt and jacket aside to reveal another amulet, this one depicting the scroll of Saint Fabia.

"That is downright peculiar. Clerics don't normally carry the tokens of other orders. And the Mithrite's don't have female priests." Tia glanced at Frederick. "Did Miriam name her sect?"

Frederick shook his head. "Nah. I just saw her the one time."

"I thought she belonged to Saint Andrew," said Bert, "seeing as she moved into their old abbey."

This makes no sense. Why would a priestess of Fabia be carrying a Mithraic relic and move into a monastery dedicated to Saint Andrews? Was she an imposter?

Tia looked at Kyle. "Did she tell you anything?"

Kyle's face scrunched. Then he let out a sigh. "Just to stop drinking." His brow furrowed. "She's a sorceress, though."

Peter drained his cup. "We must be underway."

Tia continued to worry over the puzzle as the carriage rolled towards Cosslet. Sister Miriam, a priestess of Fabia, arrived in Cosslet two weeks earlier, bearing a potent token of Saint Mithras. The Mithrite's didn't accept women as clergy. So, how had she obtained it? And why had she separated the talisman?

The solution hit her with such force she sat erect – to hide it. From whom? Silam. The sorcerer knew of the dagger and considered it a threat. An image of the massacre at the Boundary tree popped into Tia's mind. There'd been a woman among the dead, wearing a dark hooded robe and white scarf that could be mistaken for a cleric's cassock. "Couldn't tell a priestess from a peasant."

"What was that my lady," asked Frederick. "You seem frightened."

"Just thinking aloud." Tia made a dismissive wave. 'Priests from peasants.' The Chou man had said that. Another memory came to her: two clerics running along a rain-drenched road, one pausing to offer a word of warning. "Beware." They'd tried to warn her.

"What?" Frederick leaned towards her.

"The massacre at the Boundary Tree," said Tia, only semi-aware of the query. "The demon was after Sister Miriam. But in the rain, it mistook the peasants for priests, and killed them instead."

Dead silence followed her words. Tia realized everybody in the carriage save the still slumbering Rebecca was staring at her.

"Bad business then and worse later." Frederick fell back in his seat. "Best not to speak of such things."

The journey continued in silence.

The carriage burst from the forest into a realm lit by the last rays of a bloody sun. Distant howls from the forest sent a jolt through Tia's frame.

"The devil is emptying hell of ghouls and ghosts." Frederick peered through the window. "I don't care for the look of those clouds, either."

"There's still light," said Garret.

Frederick looked at him. "Not much. And the shadows are getting longer. Twilight is almost upon us."

Kyle must have realized this as well, for the carriage increased its speed, veritably flying across a landscape of fallow fields and puddles of water.

They rattled across the bridge and into Cosslet. Through the hatch, Tia glimpsed tendrils of mist winding through town, half obscuring its buildings. The village felt cold and dead.

"It looks deserted," said Garret.

"Maybe that bastard killed everybody." Worry played across Frederic's features.

"No," said Tia with a confidence she didn't feel.

The wagon halted before the church. Sir Peter appeared in the window. "Remain here." He dismounted and went inside.

Minutes ticked by each a small eon. Tia's gaze didn't waver from the entrance. The prayers imbued in its foundation offered the best protection from the spirits soon to be abroad.

The church door burst open. Peter stormed towards the coach; face contorted in anger. "It's no good. We'll have to trust to the keep."

Tia didn't dare ask what Peter found in the shrine.

The wagon clattered into the keep yard. If Cosslet felt deserted, the keep appeared downright haunted. Tia half-expected to glimpse ghosts in the windows.

The refugees entered the keep with the measured paces of the condemned. To Tia, the castle felt dead and abandoned. Her skin chilled as she entered.

Celina ascended the stairs without a word or glance at the others. Kyle placed logs and tinder in the fireplace and ignited them with an incantation.

Peter wandered into the kitchen and emerged clenching a bottle and five cups which he placed on the table without a word.

Tia filled each glass, claimed one, and took a sip. The wine was flat, bitter. She wanted to spit it out. Instead, she swallowed.

Kyle sat alone, staring at nothing. His cup remained untouched.

Bert drained his cup in a single gulp, then stared silently at nothing.

Peter emptied his glass and sat and faced the fire. Tia sat next to him and watched the flames leap and crackle. Rebecca, carried in by Kyle, sprawled across a cushioned bench, writhing in tortured slumber.

Outside, the hell winds built with fierce intensity. Thuds and pops announced the impact of airborne objects against the walls. The keeps stones creaked and groaned. The sound of breaking glass from an overhead window reached Tia's ears. Moments later a massive tree branch bounced to the floor amidst a cascade of crystalline fragments.

They all stared at the log. "I have a bad feeling about this," said Frederick. Nobody disputed him.

A huge gust slammed into the keep. So many objects struck in such rapid succession the walls vibrated. It felt as though they were inside a giant drum.

Frederick shouted and pointed a spiderweb of cracks across the hall.

Tia's eyes widened as stones popped from the bulwark.

"Tia, move!" Peter shouted. He ran towards Tia, pointing frantically at the ceiling.

Tia jumped from her chair an instant before a slab of masonry smashed it to splinters. Water cascaded from above, turning the floor into a puddle. A gust of wind extinguished every candle in the room and dimmed the fireplace to embers. Ominous creaks and groans sounded from the upper walls and ceiling.

Tia wrapped her arms around Peter. "This place isn't safe!"

"The servant's bunkhouse!" Kyle pointed at the door. "It's sturdier."

"That means crossing the courtyard." Thunderous bursts punctuated Peter's statement.

Wood screeched as a beam in the ceiling tore loose.

Frederick flung the door open to fierce wind and pounding rain.

Kyle scooped up Rebecca as though she weighed nothing and stumbled towards the door.

"Stay together!" Peter ordered. He kept his right arm draped across Tia's shoulder.

"Where's Celina?" shouted Tia.

Peter stopped. "She's upstairs. I'll get her. Go!" He shoved Tia at the door. "Stay behind Kyle!"

Tia stumbled into the storm. She couldn't see a thing. The wind pushed at her. Its roar filled her ears. Then something heavy knocked her to the ground. Groping hands helped Tia to her feet. Then the wind fell away. Kyle's voice rang out, and flame ignited in a fireplace, revealing a stone chamber lined with benches.

Tia plopped on the nearest bench and took a breath. Her side ached.

Beside her, Garret, Bert, and Fredrick did the same. Kyle stared at the fire.

The door banged open. Peter entered amidst a howling gust, carrying Celina, who clenched a canvas square.

"She was painting," said Peter. "She didn't stop even when half the ceiling collapsed."

Tia stared past Peter at the keep, a black shape against a dark sky. Groans and pops filled the air. The whole structure trembled.

"It's about to cave-in," shouted Fredric.

Kyle stood and threw his weight against the door, forcing it towards the latch.

Then Cosslet keep collapsed in on itself.

Celina dropped the painting, opened her mouth. "My home is gone."

Tia eyed the wreckage. "My things are in there." She couldn't hear herself above the racket.

"We're alive," said Peter. "That's what counts."

Peter joined Kyle. Together, they pushed the door shut. The noise subsided.

Tia found Celina's canvas next to her. She picked it up. "Oh, God no." Silam's image stared back at her.

"What's all the racket about?" Rebecca sat and rubbed her eyes.

EMPIRE: COUNTRY XXIV – Li-Pang

Li-Pang the chill spring air as he skipped along the road. He'd finished another winter at Putlog's school. Now, Reed Village awaited his return.

Li-Pang mentally reviewed the village girls as he dodged puddles and ice patches. Po-Sun? Pretty, but she had other suitors. Wei-Tang enjoyed his music, but also possessed a mercurial temperament.

Brush snapped in the woods. The on Li-Pang's neck rose. His skin prickled. Danger. He faced the sound and focused.

Li-Pang didn't know another word that suited his strange knack, which let him see things that were far off – or hidden. What the focus revealed made him gasp: Vree!

An entire pack of the vermin!

One vree alone was a nuisance. Li-Pang might deter two or even three of the dog-sized beasts with his staff, though the venom-tipped tentacles presented a hazard. But now an entire pack confronted him. So, the choice was 'run or die.' So, Li-Pang ran.

Brush rustled ahead of Li-Pang. A large vree, almost mule-sized, stepped onto the road. He glanced over his shoulder: three more of the creatures followed him.

Li Pang charged into the undergrowth. He twisted through close-set saplings and skirted the denser clumps of brush at almost a dead run. But the vree did not relinquish their pursuit.

The vegetation stopped. Li-Pang stood, windmilling his arms at the brink of a narrow gorge. Water gurgled in its bottom.

Li-Pang considered the crevice. Could he leap it? Slathering sounds announced the vree's imminent arrival. He backed three paces and selected a deadfall that reached into the gap. Then he ran. Branches slapped at him. He was through the brush. His heart raced as he kicked off the log. Below, rocks projected from the water, resembling a monster waiting to devour him. The gully's far side rushed at him. Then agony erupted in his shins as he struck the opposite side.

Li-Pang grabbed a drooping branch and pulled himself to safety. Pain stabbed through his legs when he moved.

The lead vree reached the chasm and issued a gurgling howl at its prey. Then it leaped. Li-Pang watched it strike the cliff, scramble for purchase, and fall into the water where it vanished.

Hope surged in Li-Pang's breast. Then it faded as the remaining vree negotiated a path along the chasm's rim towards another fallen tree, one that spanned the gap.

Li-Pang hobbled away from the gorge. His legs throbbed. It hurt to bend his knees. It was much harder to slip between the saplings and around the brush than it had been.

The vegetation vanished, replaced by a vista of churning water with fallow plots on the opposite shore. He knew those fields: they butted against Reed Villages western side. He was almost home. And doomed because the swollen river was too cold and furious to swim.

Li-Pang remembered that Ho Sin had slipped into the water and drowned near this very spot – and he'd been a renowned swimmer.

A slathering howl announced the vree's imminent arrival. Li-Pang considered the bank. He could slide down it to the water's edge, but what then?

"Step." The faint voice spoke into his left ear.

Li-Pang glanced frantically in different directions and saw nobody. "Who are you?"

"Step."

A notion occurred to Li-Pang. His gaze settled on a shadow that stretched across the slab. A shadow with no source. Li-Pang remembered that entity, though he'd seldom glimpsed it since Nan-Tang's years-ago humiliation.

The dark phantasm's insubstantial limb stretched across the river. "Focus. Step. Shadow."

Li-Pang gulped. Dare he trust this insubstantial entity? Thrashing sounds in the brush told him he had no choice. He placed a tentative foot on the black shape.

Brush snapped behind Li-Pang. The vree arrived.

Li-Pang stared at the far bank, integrating the shadow and the river. "Focus. Remember."

Li-Pang's gaze settled on a rocky grotto he'd frequented. He visualized the ash ring that never washed away, and the crude graffiti marks scrawled on the stones.

"Step."

Eyes focused on the grotto, Li-Pang stepped from the precipice and into a realm of black and white and gray that flashed past him in mere heartbeats.

Claws and tentacles lashed at the spot where he'd been standing an instant earlier.

Li-Pang blinked. His feet felt wobbly. He was ravenous. Slowly he turned and saw the vree standing on the far side of the river, staring at him.

EMPIRE: COUNTRY XXV - Tia

Tia awoke to soft lyre music in a small, sparse, and chill room. She sat and shook her head.

Li-Pang. Again, Tia dreamed a snippet of the strange man's life. That trick of his – that 'focus' – was sorcery, plain and simple. Other magicians employed the same spell – even that oaf Kyle. Had Li-Pang gone on to study wizardry? And what of the shadow creature? That entity raised goosebumps on her arms. It was evil.

Rebecca sat her instrument on a nightstand. "Shall I make you presentable, my lady?"

"Yes, please. One must maintain appearances." Tia rubbed her eyes. "It wouldn't do to disappoint Consul Andric."

A thoughtful expression appeared on Rebecca's face as she produced a brush. "Still having the dreams?"

Tia plopped in a hard chair and pressed a hand to her forehead. "They never stop. Sometimes I fear the world itself is but a dream."

"I know the feeling." Rebecca stood behind Tia and ran the brush through Tia's locks. Rebecca claimed to remember nothing of either the theatrical performance or horrible ritual in the woods. Tia believed her, wanted to believe her – but those gypsies belonged to her clan. And gypsies lied. So, believing Rebecca's tale was a calculated risk. But one that Tia took anyway.

Hair styled, Tia and Rebecca ventured into the Manor's halls. She found Acting Consul Andric perusing a sheaf of papers in the dining room.

Sigrid's cousin was short, plump, round-faced, and pug-nosed, the very image of a beloved grandfather. He'd been watching Liam when Sigrid attended Silam's performance, hence his survival.

The Acting Consul's eyes stared at her over a pair of reading glasses. "I trust you slept well, Lady Tia."

"I did. Your gracious hospitality is appreciated, Consul Andric." Tia forced a smile to her lips. Formalities mattered. They provided a barrier between her and the horrors of Hell Night.

Andric placed the documents on the table. "Sir Cortez brought these by a short while ago. He salvaged them from the ruin of his brother's castle. We must discuss them after breakfast."

So, Lupton's new ruler had discovered the agreement she'd forged with Ian. Likely, he'd try to claim the fumar trees for Lupton. "Certainly, Consul." Tia reclined on a couch. "Did Sir Cortez bring any news of Lord Charles whereabouts?"

"He pursues a lead as we speak." Andric didn't sound optimistic.

"Any news from Cosslet?"

"Their mood remains glum." The villagers not abducted by Silam's henchmen spent that evening in tormented slumber. They'd awakened to a reality where their neighbors and kin were dead.

"Has Kyle returned yet?" He'd been dispatched yesterday to Stone Hollow to alert the authorities. Tia fervently hoped he wasn't lying dead in a ditch.

"I'm afraid not."

Celina and Liam strode into the room, arms intertwined and heads together. They loaded themselves onto a single couch as a female servant entered, bearing a large tray laden with bread, bowls of gruel, and sliced fruit.

Andric claimed the master's couch while Rebecca took a perch in the corner, strumming a quiet instrumental piece. She would dine later in the kitchen.

Breakfast finished, Tia retired with Andric to the study, where portraits of former consuls frowned over musty furnishings. There, they went over the agreement she'd made with Ian. Andric surprised Tia: he did claim the fumar forest for Lupton but recognized her family's expertise at raising such an extraordinary crop. Neither brought up Brutus. That could wait.

"So, partnership, then," asked Tia.

"Yes. We can draw the papers later today." The Consul tilted his head and sneezed, followed by a racking cough.

"My lord, are you alright?"

Andric raised a hand. "Dratted sniffles. They drain the life right out of me." He sneezed again. "I shall take a cordial."

Tia knew the potion would put Andric straight to sleep. "I shall prepare a preliminary agreement."

"Tank you."

Tia watched Andric exit the chamber, leaving her alone in the study.

Preparing the partnership papers took Tia back in time to her university days, when she'd sat hunched over a slate in Professor Fulton's class, listening to that white-haired worthy drone on about clauses and clarifications. That lore permeated Tia's brain: a single effort sufficed to produce a document that would satisfy both Andric and her parents. Satisfying Brutus would be another matter.

Paper's drafted, Tia turned her attention to the remaining manuscripts. One pile came from Cosslet. The remainder belonged to the former Consul.

Tia had a puzzle to solve. Sister Miriam. Silam. Those two had a history. Tia intended to discover it. She opened a tome with the Cortez stamp across its spine. Ian's neat handwriting stared back at her. Tia recoiled as if physically struck.

"I need answers." She forced herself to read the text – a daybook, the dull life of a country nobleman. She read pages of livestock counts and crop figures, interspersed with references and anecdotes about neighboring lords. A name caught her eye: Lord Osmic, aka Lord Lard. Her third suitor.

Tia blinked and read the entry. In it, Lord Osmic described a fire that destroyed the village of Oak Hill. She paused and tapped the table. Yes, the obese aristocrat had been preoccupied with that tragedy during her brief visit. He'd seemed genuinely concerned about the town's plight, moaning the blaze killed a dozen people and destroyed thirty buildings – including the sole theater in the region. Pieces clicked in Tia's mind. Theater. Silam's murderous band, masquerading as a troupe of entertainers.

"It was supposed to be Oak Hill." She flopped back in the chair. But the fire altered Silam's plan. Cosslet became Silam's second choice. But what started the conflagration? Tia sat straight in her seat. Not 'what.' 'Who.' Sister Miriam. The priestess thwarted the sorcerer's ritual by burning the town.

Tia returned her attention to the entry. The fire claimed a dozen lives – a fraction of the number slaughtered at Fort Cragmoor. Osmic inquired if Baron Cortez would accept survivors from the destroyed settlement. Ian responded he would accept the refugees, then went on to name a dozen vacant farmsteads that could be resettled – including five at Groveton.

Tia continued her perusal and encountered another familiar name: Lord Cassidy, aka Lord Tombstone. That dour soul complained about the theft of artifacts from his family's crypts. Tia paused a second time. Yes, Lord Tombstone had mentioned the incident during her stay. But most of his discourse centered on the prowess of those ancestors. Perhaps one had returned home with a certain bronze ritual knife? Ian's curt entry provided no clues.

The last page began with Tia's arrival in the barony. Unable to bear reading Ian's assessment of her, Tia closed the book and opened a tome with Lupton's mark on the cover. She read dull notations on country life interspersed with aristocratic gossip, most from the eastern empire. The entry almost slipped past her, but the name caught Tia's eye: a

'Sister Mariam' and unnamed lay brother taking up residence at the ruined Saint Andrew's Abbey.

Ok, lets puzzle this through. Sister Miriam has a secret war with Silam. She thwarted Silam in Oak Hill by burning the town, but realized she needed something special to destroy the conjurors pet – and the conjuror himself. Somehow, she knew Lord Cassidy counted an enchanted dagger amongst his collection – so she stole it. Then, the priestess established herself in Lupton District. But why separate the weapon's parts? Why give the hilt to Father Barnabas? He wasn't even a warrior like Peter, let alone a Mithrite. Tia tapped the table. The knife needed a competent wielder. It needed Peter. Likely, Barnabas would have given the talisman to Sir Cortez once he'd been appointed Sheriff – Saint Mithras being a champion of law and order. That fit. But why give the blade to the woodworker? Had Anatoly intended it for Celina's toy knight? Would that have brought it to Peter? It seemed unlikely. Instead, he'd attached it to one of Silam's puppets. And it was mere unforeseeable chance that Peter had been tossed into the same wagon as that puppet. Tia frowned and tapped the table. The whole approach seemed ridiculously convoluted. How could Miriam be so certain the pieces would come together in the right hands when needed? That would have required knowledge of the future. Tia sat straight. "Sister Miriam isn't just a priestess with a knack for sorcery. She is a prophet." Fortune tellers and petty diviners filled market squares across the Empire, their predictions almost always rubbish, but rarely there'd be one who truly could glimpse the future. Sister Miriam must be one of them.

"Brainy and beautiful." A hand clamped over Tia's lips.

Tia's eyes widened. Her heart almost stopped beating. Charles! Tia bit the digits blocking her mouth.

"Bitch!"

Agony exploded in Tia's skull as her head slammed into the desk. Tia screamed in pain and anger. She hurled herself sideways.

Charles grabbed Tia's wrist and twisted her arm so that she faced him. "Surprised to see me?" Charles smiled beneath a layer of dirt. He wore rough peasant's garb, covered with grime and leaves. "You shouldn't be. I know every secret of both castles – including where the slip-me-outs are located."

Tia screamed.

"Oh, enough of that. Nobody will hear you. The Consul's liked their privacy." Charles' eyes darted from side to side as he spoke. His free hand clenched a dagger.

A semblance of thought returned to Tia. "You're a wanted man. Why come back?"

"Because He wants you dead."

Tia's heart raced. "You're talking about Silam."

"Don't say that name!" Charles' voice rose to a shrill pitch.

Tia kicked the renegade's leg and hurled herself at him. They crashed into the bookshelf. Tomes spilled to the floor.

"You bitch!" Charles rose, brandishing the blade.

Tia sat on the floor, eyes fixed on the knife, unable to move.

"Lady Tia?" Kyle's voice penetrated the thick wood.

"Help!" The shout took all of Tia's energy.

The door burst clear from its frame. Charles pivoted to avoid its falling bulk, knife flashing at Kyle's burly form.

Kyle's fist slammed into Charles face and knocked him into the wall.

The Forester remained erect but wobbled on his feet.

Kyle struck him a second time. The knife dropped to the carpet, along with its owner.

A man dressed in gold and purple of an imperial functionary entered the office. "I am – good God, what happened here?"

Tia stood and pointed at the Forester. "That's him – Charles Cortez, the man behind the murders."

The newcomer stared at Charles. "Why'd he come here?"

Charles stirred.

Tia took a step back.

"Quick. Bind him." The official motioned at the door. Two men in imperial armor entered the room. One produced a pair of manacles which he slapped onto the Foresters wrists.

The functionary faced Tia. "I am Lord Barret DuPaul, an emissary of his Supremacy Morgan DuSwaimair the Second, Emperor of Solaria." He inclined his head. "You are Lady Tia Samos of Equitant." It wasn't a question.

"I am." Tia managed a stilted bow despite her shock.

Kyle plopped into a chair which creaked beneath his weight, left hand clenching a red stain on his right forearm.

The soldiers pulled the renegade to his feet. Lord Barret glared at him. "We have you, Charles Cortez. Soon, we'll have your confederate."

Charles smiled through a mask of blood and dirt. Inaudible words left his lips.

'Confederate.' The functionary meant Silam. "Lord Barret, Silam is a sorcerer of immense power."

"So am I." A man of aristocratic demeanor entered the study, head crowned in dark curls, clad in the blue and silver rune-robe of a master magus. His eyes flicked to Tia. "I am Archimage Nikolas Antigonus of the Celestial Circle."

Tia blinked. The empires premier magical practitioners belonged to the Celestial Circle.

"I am confident Master Antigonus can best this saban upstart," said Lord DuPaul.

The soldiers pulled Charles from the study.

Antigonus inspected Kyle. Crimson liquid dripped from his sleeve to the floor. "You're bleeding on the carpet."

A commotion from the hallway reached Tia's ears.

"Let me pass!" Peter burst into the room, towing a soldier with him. "Tia – you're ok!" Relief flooded his features.

Lord Barret regarded the Knight. "And you would be Sir Peter Cortez, formerly of Benedict's Bravos."

Peter's eyes flicked between Tia and the emissary. He stumbled through a greeting.

Kyle fabricated an improvised bandage with a strip torn from his shirt.

Peter faced Lord Barret. "We must get after Silam."

"No." The official raised his hand. "You – each of you – will give me a full deposition of this incident."

"Then we go after Silam?"

"No. Master Antigonus and I will search out the Saban and his confederates. You three" – he motioned at Tia, Peter, and Kyle – "will go to the Imperial Capitol with the other witnesses. The Emperor has taken a personal interest in this atrocity."

(CONTINUED IN 'EMPIRE: CAPITAL')

Also by Tim Goff

Empire
Empire: Country
Empire: Capital
Empire: Capital
Empire: Estate
Empire: Estate